"Thank you for bringing me tonight.

"I know I wasn't the person who was supposed to enjoy these things with you, and I might be wrong for feeling this way, but I'm glad I got to do them, even if I was a spare."

"There is no other woman I'd rather be here with than you, Regan."

At that precise moment he had made a decision. He wouldn't handle his intense attraction to her. He intended to act on it. There was no reason for him to continue to fight his desire for her. Regan was a grown woman who could make her own decisions about whether she would want an affair with him or not. He would never intentionally hurt her and he would be truthful about everything.

She smiled. "That's a kind thing to say, Garth."

He had a feeling she didn't believe him.

That meant he had eleven days to convince her he'd meant every word.

* * *

The Wife He Needs by Brenda Jackson is part of the Westmoreland Legacy: The Outlaws series.

**Selected praise for *New York Times* and
USA TODAY bestselling author
Brenda Jackson**

"Brenda Jackson writes romance that sizzles
and characters you fall in love with."

—*New York Times* and *USA TODAY*
bestselling author Lori Foster

"Jackson's trademark ability to weave multiple
characters and side stories together makes shocking
truths all the more exciting."

—*Publishers Weekly*

"There is no getting away from the sex appeal
and charm of Jackson's Westmoreland family."

—*RT Book Reviews* on *Feeling the Heat*

"What is it with these Westmoreland men? Each is
sexier and more charming than the one before…. Hot,
sexy, smart and romantic, this story has it all."

—*RT Book Reviews* on *The Proposal*

"Jackson has a talent for creating the sexiest men and
pairing them off against feisty females. This story has
everything a hot romance should have."

—*RT Book Reviews* on *Hot Westmoreland Nights*

"Is there anything more irresistible than
a man so in love with a woman that he's willing
to give her what she believes is her heart's desire? The
Westmoreland clan will claim even
more fans with this entry."

—*RT Book Reviews* on
What a Westmoreland Wants

BRENDA JACKSON

THE WIFE HE NEEDS

HARLEQUIN
DESIRE

If you purchased this book without a cover you should be aware
that this book is stolen property. It was reported as "unsold and
destroyed" to the publisher, and neither the author nor the
publisher has received any payment for this "stripped book."

ISBN-13: 978-1-335-20949-8

The Wife He Needs

Recycling programs
for this product may
not exist in your area.

Copyright © 2020 by Brenda Streater Jackson

All rights reserved. No part of this book may be used or reproduced in any
manner whatsoever without written permission except in the case of brief
quotations embodied in critical articles and reviews.

This is a work of fiction. Names, characters, places and incidents
are either the product of the author's imagination or are used fictitiously.
Any resemblance to actual persons, living or dead, businesses,
companies, events or locales is entirely coincidental.

This edition published by arrangement with Harlequin Books S.A.

For questions and comments about the quality of this book,
please contact us at CustomerService@Harlequin.com.

Harlequin Enterprises ULC
22 Adelaide St. West, 40th Floor
Toronto, Ontario M5H 4E3, Canada
www.Harlequin.com

Printed in U.S.A.

Brenda Jackson is a *New York Times* bestselling author of more than one hundred romance titles. Brenda lives in Jacksonville, Florida, and divides her time between family, writing and traveling. Email Brenda at authorbrendajackson@gmail.com or visit her on her website at brendajackson.net.

Books by Brenda Jackson

Harlequin Desire

The Westmoreland Legacy

The Rancher Returns
His Secret Son
An Honorable Seduction
His to Claim
Duty or Desire

Forged of Steele

Seduced by a Steele
Claimed by a Steele

Westmoreland Legacy: The Outlaws

The Wife He Needs

Visit her Author Profile page at Harlequin.com, or brendajackson.net, for more titles.

You can also find Brenda Jackson on Facebook, along with other Harlequin Desire authors, at Facebook.com/harlequindesireauthors!

To the man who will always and forever be
the love of my life, Gerald Jackson, Sr.

Hatred stirreth up strifes:
but love covereth all sins.
—*Proverbs* 10:12

One

"So, when is the wedding, Garth?"

Garth Outlaw raised his eyes from studying his cards. Was his brother playing mind games to mess with his concentration?

"And just what wedding are you talking about?"

Garth glanced around the table and saw the smirks on the faces of all four of his brothers. Even Jess had made a trip home from the nation's capital for a week long visit.

"Is anyone going to answer?" Garth asked.

Jess grinned as he threw out a card. "I heard it from Dad the moment I walked through the door. He claims you've gotten over Karen Piccard, decided to settle down and do whatever needs to be done for the benefit of the company, which includes getting a wife and making babies to guarantee the Outlaw dynasty. Those were his words, not mine."

"We heard the same thing," Cash said, with Sloan and Maverick nodding in agreement.

Garth didn't say anything. Being the oldest son of Bartram "Bart" Outlaw wasn't easy, especially when his father liked spreading information that wasn't true. However, in this case, it was. At least partly. He was planning to do what needed to be done for the company. But he seriously doubted he would ever get over Karen. She would always have his heart.

"No wedding date has been set because I haven't chosen a bride."

His brother Cash sat up straight in his chair. "Are you really thinking about settling down with a wife and making babies?" he asked, as if the thought of doing such a thing was as unheard of as living in outer space.

Garth threw out some chips. "Why not? I don't see any of you guys rushing to the altar to continue the Outlaw legacy. Not even you, Jess, and you're the politician in the family. You of all people should be thinking about acquiring a wife." A couple of years ago, Jess had gotten elected as a senator from Alaska.

A grin touched Jess's lips. "No, thank you. I'm not ready to fall in love."

Garth shrugged. "Who said anything about falling in love?"

"You're thinking of marrying a woman you don't love?" This question came from Sloan.

"For me there's no other way."

There was no reason to explain what he meant. They knew.

"And you'll do it because Bart says it needs to be done?"

Garth rolled his eyes at his youngest brother, Maverick, who'd been quiet up to now. "No, I'll consider doing it because I think it's about time I settled down. I'm thirty-eight, and dating gets old."

"Speak for yourself," Maverick said, grinning. "I happen to enjoy dating a lot of women."

Garth shook his head. "And Walker got me thinking. Look how long he was a loner before he got married. If he can do it, then anyone can."

Walker Rafferty was Garth's best friend. A couple of years ago, Walker had met his current wife and now they were parents to twins, a boy and a girl they'd named Walker and Westlyn. Nobody thought Walker would ever remarry after losing his first wife and son in a car accident. Surprisingly, ten years later, Walker had fallen in love again. Garth was happy for Walker, and inspired to settle down, but honestly, he couldn't see himself falling in love. He was convinced Karen was the only woman he was meant to love.

He and Karen had met in the Marines. They'd fallen in love immediately and made plans to marry after their enlistment. They'd dated six months and then one morning during a routine border check in Syria, her military chopper had crashed, killing everyone on board. He'd never even gotten the chance to bring Karen to Fairbanks and introduce the woman he'd loved to his family.

"Walker certainly does seem a lot happier these days, thanks to our cousin," Cash said, intruding into Garth's thoughts.

Garth nodded as he studied his cards. Yes, Walker had become the Outlaws' cousin-in-law after marrying Bailey Westmoreland. Bailey was a cousin they hadn't known existed until it was proven that the Westmorelands and the Outlaws were related. The physical resemblance between the two families could not be disputed, although for some reason their father still would not accept the fact that the Outlaws and Westmorelands were kin. However, like Garth and his siblings had told Bart, it didn't matter whether or not he accepted the kinship, it was the truth.

The Westmoreland extended family spread from Georgia and Texas to Montana, Colorado and California. After growing up with no other relatives, it was fun joining the Westmorelands whenever they had get-togethers or family events, like the annual Westmoreland Charity Ball in Denver. Garth loved it whenever the Westmorelands and the Outlaws got together.

Hours later, after the poker game ended with Cash winning all their money, everyone retired to bed except for Garth and Jess. Although all six Outlaw offspring owned homes in Fairbanks, every once in a while, to appease the old man, they would stay under his roof at the Outlaw Estates.

Some people found it amazing that the six Outlaw siblings were as close as they were, considering each one of them had a different mother. Unfortunately, some of those women had turned out to be gold diggers. When the divorces became final, Bart's attorneys made sure he was given full custody of his children.

Garth was the oldest. His mother had been Bart's first wife and had come from a wealthy family. She had married Bart against her parents' wishes. And when her family finally got to her, she had asked Bart for a divorce. He told her he would give her one but she couldn't take his child. In the end, she'd left without Garth. She'd remarried a couple years later, to the man her parents had chosen. After marrying her second husband, Juanita pretty much forgot Garth existed. However, his maternal grandparents had left him a pretty hefty trust fund when they'd died twenty or so years ago.

Jessup or Jess, as he preferred to be called, was thirty-six and the second oldest, and had always wanted a career in politics. Jess's mother, Joyce, had been the first gold digger, and Bart had ended his marriage to Joyce before their first anniversary rolled around. Bart had taken her to court for custody of Jess.

Cashen, who was usually called Cash, was thirty-four and the third-born son. Cash's mother, Ellen, had been a decent woman and Bart's third wife. In a way, she'd been too decent for Bart. She was soft-spoken and had tried bringing out the good in Bart. When she'd realized such a thing wasn't possible, she'd left. Even with Bart's threats, Ellen had called Bart's bluff and tried to take Cash with her. In the end, she'd lost the custody fight after finding out Bart had friends in high places.

Sloan was thirty-two. His mother, Barbie, had been

another one who'd picked Bart for his money. Although the marriage had lasted less than six months, that was long enough for Sloan to be conceived. Barbie'd had no problem leaving Sloan behind—for the right amount— when she split. She hadn't been seen or heard from again.

Maverick, at twenty-nine, was the youngest Outlaw son and the most womanizing. Granted, all of them enjoyed their share of the opposite sex from time to time, but Maverick had his share and then some. His mother had been an exploiter, too. Rosalind was the one who'd been caught having an affair right under Bart's nose. However, there hadn't been any question that Maverick was Bart's kid, since he favored the old man more than any of them. Right down to the cleft in his chin.

Last but certainly not least, was Bart's only daughter, definitely his pride and joy, twenty-five-year-old Charm. To this day, Charm's mother, Claudia, was the only woman Bart had ever loved and the one he couldn't handle. And…she'd been the only one Bart hadn't married, but not for lack of trying.

Claudia had refused to accept Bart's marriage proposals. All five of them. The most recent was four years ago, when Charm had turned twenty-one. The Outlaws saw Claudia frequently because, unlike the other mothers, she had an open invitation to visit as often as she liked, but she never visited as often as Bart would have wanted. Claudia didn't tolerate Bart's grouchiness and seemed to bring out the best in Bart…if there was such a thing.

Bart hadn't known Claudia was pregnant when their

affair had ended. She'd left for parts unknown. Fifteen years later, Claudia reappeared with Charm in tow, telling Bart she couldn't handle Charm's sassiness anymore and for him to now deal with it.

Unfortunately, Bart dealt with it the wrong way by spoiling Charm even more rotten. It had taken the five older brothers stepping in and applying the firm hand their father had refused to apply. In the end, their spoiled sister had settled down. That didn't mean she didn't try their patience every once in a while, because she did.

"So, what's the real deal with you and this marriage thing, Garth?" Jess asked, intruding into Garth's thoughts. "Unlike what Dad thinks, I find it hard to believe you've gotten over Karen…although it has been close to ten years now."

Garth glanced over at Jess as he took a sip of his wine. Garth was close to all his siblings, but there was a special closeness between him and Jess. Jess had confided his intentions to Garth when he'd decided to run for United States senator. Jess had won the election in a landslide victory. And he knew just what Karen had meant to Garth, because it was all in the letters Garth would write home to Jess.

Garth leaned back in his chair. "It could be twenty years and I still won't get over Karen, Jess. I loved her too much. But I'm not getting any younger, and I want the same happiness I see that Walker and our cousins have. Besides," he said with a chuckle, "I figure if I make the first step, the rest of you will follow suit."

Jess threw his head back and laughed. "Don't expect

that to happen. Some of us aren't ready for home, hearth and the sound of little feet yet." Then Jess added, "Now that you've made up your mind, have you decided on a particular woman? Anyone we know?"

Garth shook his head. "Nope. Taking Charm's advice, I—"

"Wait! Hold up. You took Charm's advice about something?"

Garth chuckled. "Yes. I know it sounds scary, but I liked what she suggested. It's a totally different approach to meeting a woman who is wife material."

"What approach is that?" Jess asked, taking a sip of his beer.

"A private dating service."

Jess nearly choked. "You're serious?"

Garth smiled. "Yes. I thought it was way out there at first, too, until Charm convinced me how productive it would be. She did all the legwork for me and found this high-class dating agency that's located in Beverly Hills, California. Just to be considered as an applicant the men must have a specified financial portfolio, and the women are required to not only be attractive but have a certain level of poise, education, classiness and sophistication."

Shifting in his seat, Garth added. "I further specified I wanted a woman who was trustworthy, had good morals and was one who wants to become a wife and mother one day. Sooner than later. And she must share my interests and hobbies. I provided a list of them."

"Have they found such a paragon of a woman who met all your specifications?"

Garth grinned. "Surprisingly, yes. Trust me, any woman who comes through this particular dating service is well vetted. She'll keep things confidential and private during the entire process."

"Have you met her yet?"

"No, but she has agreed to spend two weeks with me, at a location we both agreed to, so we can get to know each other better. Of course, I'm covering all the expenses, including those to get her there."

"And exactly where is *there*?"

"Santa Cruz, Spain. I'm flying there next week."

"This method sounds so impersonal. More like a business arrangement."

"In a way, it is. I'm hiring the service to match me with someone who's compatible with my needs and desires. I've seen pictures of her and she's beautiful, and her résumé is impressive. If things work out the way I'm hoping they will, after our Spain trip we'll continue to date and then eventually talk marriage."

"A loveless marriage."

"Yes, a loveless marriage. I will honor her, respect her and take care of all her needs, but I won't ever love her," Garth said bluntly. "I'll be honest and forthright with her about that, Jess. I won't have her entering the marriage with false hope or illusions."

"Why use a dating service? I would think you're capable of finding a woman on your own."

"Didn't have time."

"Any reason you're in a rush?" Jess asked.

"No."

Jess studied him intently and Garth wished he

wouldn't do that. Jess could always figure out his mo-
tives, and Garth hoped like hell that he didn't figure out
this one. The less Jess knew, the better.

"Well, you're an ace when it comes to strategic planning, and I wish you the best. I hope the woman is everything you want, Garth, and things work out."

"Thanks, Jess. I hope so, too."

Regan Fairchild's job as a corporate pilot was one
that anyone who enjoyed flying would love. Then why
was she thinking of leaving it? The answer to her question was the gorgeous specimen of a man walking toward the plane with his briefcase in one hand and a cell
phone in the other. His long black coat whipped against
his legs as he headed toward the plane while ignoring
the strong gust of Alaskan wind that always accompanied October weather. The shoulders beneath the coat
were massive and powerful, which gave him a totally
heart-stopping, virile look.

He was handsome, and she was convinced that in
another life he'd been an explorer, discovering and in-
vading new territories. He was always busy. He always
had a plan. He rarely slowed down, and lately he rarely
dated.

Her heart pounded in her chest like it always did
whenever she saw him. How long had it been since she'd
fallen hopelessly in love with Garth Bartram Outlaw?
Had it been ten years ago on her eighteenth birthday,
when he'd flown her and two of her besties to Las Vegas
as a high school graduation gift? Or had it been at sixteen, when he had helped her father surprise her with a

"sweet-sixteen" party at Disney World? Deep down she knew it didn't matter when it had happened. The key thing was that it *had* happened, and she needed to do something about it before Garth became her downfall.

Regan knew that as much as she wished otherwise, realistically, quitting her job was not an option. Her father, Franklin Fairchild, had been the corporate pilot for Outlaw Freight Lines for over forty years. When he retired a few years ago, she had taken over. She loved her job. She also loved the man who was headed toward her with a huge smile on his face. He did that whenever he saw her. She'd rarely known a time when Garth hadn't given her a smile. It was a smile that meant everything to her.

She knew Garth's smile was a natural part of his makeup. He rarely frowned, and when he did, everyone knew there would be trouble. He was an astute businessman, and the company had grown in leaps and bounds since he'd taken over from his father. It wasn't that Bart Outlaw hadn't been good at his work, but Garth's approach was a lot different from his father's. Bart ruled with a hard hand and was distrustful by nature. He was hard-nosed and inflexible. On the other hand, Garth knew the art of compromising, and he was also brilliant. Everybody liked Garth, and she of all people knew how easy he was to love.

She also knew about that period of sadness in his life when he'd returned home from a stint abroad as a marine. He had come back a broken man, after the woman he loved had been killed. For a while there had not been any smiles, and he'd thrown himself into working beside his father to make the company bigger and bigger.

Then, when Bart retired, or more specifically when the company's board threatened to oust him, it was Garth who'd taken over and put in all those long hours, sometimes without a social life, to pull the company through difficult times. Regan guessed that he'd also been trying to rid himself of the pain of losing the person he'd loved. More than once, she had walked in on him unexpectedly, in one of his quiet moments, to see grief in his eyes.

"Good morning, Regan," he said now, when he came to a stop in front of her.

She tilted her head back to look up at him. He was tall, but the first things that caught her attention were Garth's handsome features. Namely his smooth, coffee-and-cream complexion, piercing dark brown eyes, a perfectly shaped nose, a pair of full lips and a sculpted chin. He garnered plenty of feminine attention no matter where he went.

"Same to you, Garth. Ready to fly?" She knew she would be flying him to Santa Cruz, Spain.

"I'm ready whenever you are, and how's Franklin?"

"Dad is fine."

"Good. I need to check up on him soon. Maybe even pay him a visit."

Her father was close to all Bart's offspring but would admit that Garth had always been his favorite. Franklin had been working as Bart's pilot when Garth was born. When Bart had gained full custody of Garth, oftentimes Garth and his nanny had accompanied Bart when he traveled extensively.

"I miss him."

Regan missed her father, too. She hadn't been surprised when her father had left the cold state of Alaska to move to Florida upon retirement. He was enjoying sunshine nearly all year round.

"Everything is in order, Garth, and we'll be taking off soon."

Less than twenty minutes later, she was cruising the skies. They would make a couple of pit stops to refuel before reaching Santa Cruz. She'd never been there but had heard it was beautiful. One thing she did in addition to studying the layout of the private airport of any destination was get familiar with the area. The plan for this trip was for her to drop him off and return to get him in two weeks. She had two rest days before flying back to Alaska and would use them to get in as much sightseeing and shopping as she could. Depending on his business plans, there were times when he asked her to remain with him during the entire trip as his private chauffeur. He hadn't asked for that on this trip.

"Mind if I join you?"

She smiled. "Sure."

It wouldn't be the first time Garth had joined her in the cockpit, claiming he was bored in the seating area. Although calling it a seating area was an understatement when this jet included luxurious sleeping quarters as well as an office.

Out of the corner of her eye she saw how easily he slid into the copilot seat beside her. As usual, he smelled good. She didn't have to glance over at him to know he was gearing up with the headset. Her father had taught a teenage Garth to fly and he'd enhanced those skills while in the Marines. More than once, he'd copiloted with her on long flights.

"Estimated flight time?" he asked her.

"Twelve hours."

"First stop?"

The FAA required her to take a break after piloting for nine hours. "Bolungarvik, Iceland," she replied.

He nodded. "Nice place. I visited there a few years ago while in the Marines. It's a beautiful coastal fishing town with breathtaking scenery. Especially the mountains surrounding the harbor."

"Sounds gorgeous."

"It is."

She eased the jet into a glide while moving around a huge mountain. "You're good at that, Regan," he said.

"Thanks. I was trained by the best."

She considered her father the best pilot there was, and he'd made sure she'd gotten her private pilot license at sixteen. Her mother had died of an aneurysm when Regan was five. She and her father had a close relationship, and she missed him now that he was in Florida. However, she'd understood him wanting to spend his later years in a warmer climate. When he had sold her childhood home, he'd split the proceeds with her. She'd taken the money and purchased a home on the Tanana River.

Because Fairbanks had a military base, most of the men she'd dated had been soldiers. All were nice guys, and although she'd enjoyed their company, she hadn't gotten serious about any of them. At least not as serious as some of them had liked. Earlier in the year, she had broken up with Craig Foster. They'd dated for six months and then he'd developed jealous tendencies she hadn't cared to deal with.

"I love being up here."

She knew what he meant. There was just something about being in the beautiful blue sky, this close to heaven. "Me, too. I guess I don't have to ask if you're prepared for your meetings this trip." She knew that when it came to any business regarding Outlaw Freight Lines, Garth was always prepared.

He chuckled. "Not this trip. It's strictly for pleasure."

"Oh." Suddenly, a pain settled around her heart. That meant his two weeks in Santa Cruz would be with a woman. The thought of that bothered her even when she had no right to let it.

"No one back in Fairbanks will have need for the company jet while I'm in Santa Cruz. They have their own planes anyway," Garth said. "If you like, instead of returning to Fairbanks, you can use the time to visit your father in Florida before returning for me."

He was right; all the Outlaws had their own personal planes and could fly them. Even Charm. Due to Alaska's very limited road system, one of the most common ways of getting around was by aircraft. Locals liked to say that more Alaskans owned personal planes than cars.

"Thanks, but Dad left two days ago for a twenty-day cruise. However, if you don't mind, I'd like to spend a couple of days in Los Angeles to visit Simone." Garth knew Simone was her best friend from college.

"Of course, I don't mind. By the way, chances are we might have a guest flying back with us on the return."

Regan's stomach knotted. "A guest?"

"Yes. I'll let you know when I'm certain so you can file the proper flight information."

"All right, Garth."

The one thing Garth had never done was bring a female friend on board to spend time with him. He always kept his business and personal lives separate. But then, hadn't he said this was not a business trip?

Regan glided around another mountain and tried concentrating on piloting the plane and not on what Garth had told her. Maybe it was time for her to finally accept that the only place she had in Garth's life was this one, as his pilot. She would never be the woman who would one day wiggle her way into his heart to remove that sadness she often saw in his eyes. As much as she wished otherwise, it would never happen, and it was time for her to make her peace with that.

Two

"What do you mean she's not coming?" Garth asked, speaking into his cell phone, while rubbing a frustrated hand down his face. He had arrived in Santa Cruz expecting the woman selected by the dating service to be there already. She wasn't.

"I got a call from the dating service," Charm said. "Evidently there was some kind of mix-up in the dates. They regret their error and are hoping you will consider rescheduling."

Anger rose, heating Garth's face. A mix-up in the dates? He expected better from a company that prided itself on being the best in the business. "Since there's no reason to remain here, I'll let Regan know I'll be on the plane with her when she leaves two days from now."

"Why?"

Garth frowned. "Why what?"

"Why are you coming back home? Don't you think Cash can handle things while you're gone?"

Garth rolled his eyes. "Of course, I do. Had I thought he couldn't, I would not have left him in charge."

"Then let him do it. It will make him feel important to the company."

"He *is* important to the company, Charm. All of you are."

"Then take the time off you so rightly deserve. We've been worried about you. All those long hours you've been working over the past six months. Finalizing that Biggins deal wasn't easy, Garth. You did it and now you need some time off to enjoy yourself." She paused before adding, "I know it's disappointing not meeting your match, but look on the bright side. At least I rented a nice place for you."

Garth glanced around. Charm had made all the arrangements, and she was right. This was a nice place. It was a beautiful château in the mountains, overlooking the sea. It was spacious and the view was breathtaking. "What am I going to do here alone for two weeks?"

"Rest. Relax. Sleep. And who said you had to be alone? I booked several activities for you and your date to enjoy while in Santa Cruz. They were paid for in advance. Just ask Regan to stay and join you."

"Regan?"

"Yes, Regan."

Garth drew in a deep breath. Ever since the night of the Westmorelands' last charity ball on New Year's Eve, when he'd asked Regan to go with him upon the

Westmorelands' request, he hadn't been able to think of her in the same way. He blamed this change on the outfit she'd been wearing and the dance they'd shared. When he'd seen her and held her in his arms, desire— which he hadn't thought he was capable of feeling for any woman after Karen—had nearly driven him insane. He'd known Regan all her life and she'd been his pilot for almost five years. But on that night, he'd seen her in a whole new light.

A light he'd been trying to dim since.

"I can't invite Regan to join me at the château for two weeks, Charm."

"Why not?"

He locked his jaw for a minute, refusing to say anything that would give his sister a reason to speculate. She was the last person who needed to know of his attraction to Regan. Nor did he want her to suspect his interest in finding a wife had been driven by his attempt to end his attraction to Regan.

"I think she would prefer leaving Spain, Charm. She even mentioned visiting her girlfriend in LA."

"Trust me, Garth. Any woman would love to spend two weeks in that château. When was the last time Regan took a real vacation that didn't include visiting her father in Florida? She's been your pilot for nearly five years now, and you haven't done anything really nice for her."

He rubbed his hand down his face. "Charm, I've always done nice things for Regan."

"I mean *really* nice. She has decisions to make and…"

When Charm's voice trailed off, Garth raised a brow. "Decisions about what?"

She hesitated and he didn't like that.

"Decisions about what, Charm?" he repeated.

"I wasn't going to say anything because she told me in confidence, but maybe it's something you should know. Especially since he's offering her a lot."

Garth frowned. "What are you talking about? Who is he and what is he offering?"

When she didn't speak, he asked again, "Charm? What are you talking about?"

"You can't tell Regan I told you, but Harold Anders offered her a job as his personal pilot. The salary is good and the benefits are even better."

Garth didn't say anything as the full implications of what Charm said hit him hard. Harold Anders owned a huge computer software company in Fairbanks, with offices in Los Angeles, Dallas, Atlanta, Portland and several more cities, as well as international offices in London, Rome and Paris. He didn't have one private jet; he had several.

He also knew the man was a forty-one-year-old divorcé with a reputation for womanizing. Anders saw women as conquests and trophies, the younger the better. Garth had heard about the sex scandal involving him and his personal assistant a couple of years ago.

And he wanted Regan to be his pilot.

Anders was the last man Regan should consider working for. Besides, she worked for Garth. A Fairchild had worked for the Outlaws for over forty years. On occasion, when he traveled internationally, she was even his private chauffeur on the ground. For her to be thinking of leaving was ludicrous. He paid her a good salary and gave her generous bonuses. He wasn't complaining about the pay because he certainly felt she deserved every penny. She was valuable to him. Irreplaceable.

"I didn't say she was taking Harold Anders's offer, Garth. She has a month to decide."

"I don't like the thought that she's even considering it."

He knew the ensuing silence meant Charm didn't like it, either, but she wasn't saying anything. Charm thought of Regan like an older sister. Charm had arrived in Alaska at fifteen, full of anger and ready to take a bite out of anyone. At least anyone but Regan. The two had bonded immediately.

"I'm sure Regan won't be taking the job," Charm said. "She loves working for our company. She's said so a number of times, and I also know she enjoys flying you."

Garth wished he could be as certain of that as Charm. "Why didn't she tell me about the offer?" he asked in an annoyed tone.

"Really, Garth? She's a professional and you're her boss. She probably figured that had she mentioned it, you would have thought she was hitting you up for a raise, to counter Anders's offer."

"I would not have thought that. Besides, I'm more than her boss, Charm. Like all the Outlaws, I consider Regan a friend."

"Well, some friend you are. You'll deny her two

weeks to enjoy herself at the château with you. If I were you, I would do whatever it takes to remind her that she's not only your pilot, but also your friend."

He heard what Charm was saying; however, he wasn't sure that was a line he wanted to cross. "I don't think Regan sharing space with me here is a good idea, Charm."

"And why not?"

There was no way he would tell Charm the real reason. "I don't want her to feel uncomfortable."

"Why would she? You're overthinking things. If it was Jess, Cash, Sloan or Maverick, none of them would mind asking Regan to hang out with them for two weeks so she could have fun. I don't understand why you would have a problem with it."

"We don't have that kind of relationship."

"Well, you should. You've known her as long as they have, even longer. And everyone knows what a great bond you share with Franklin. In some ways, you're closer to him than you are to Bart."

When he didn't say anything, Charm added, "You know what I think, Garth?"

A part of him was afraid to ask. "No, what do you think?"

"I think the problem isn't with Regan but with you."

His stomach tightened. Had Charm figured out his attraction to Regan. "It's me in what way?"

"Since taking over the company you've gotten so driven to make the company successful that you've become the ultimate professional, dotting every *i* and crossing every *t*, and you've forgotten how it feels to just chill and hang out with those who remember how fun-loving you were before becoming Mr. CEO. You've become a stuffed shirt."

"A stuffed shirt?"

"Yes, and a stick-in-the-mud, too. I hate to see you become another Bart."

Garth frowned. "That won't ever happen."

"It will if you don't learn how to relax, have fun and enjoy spending time with people you can trust. If you prefer, I can take time off and fly out and spend time with you in Santa Cruz."

That was the last thing he wanted. Charm would drive him batty. "I'll ask Regan about it today."

"Good. Now about your match from the dating service. Do you want me to reschedule your time with her?"

He inhaled deeply. Maybe her not showing up was an omen. If he was honest with himself, he would admit he preferred meeting women the traditional way. "No. Please cancel my relationship with the service."

"Are you sure?"

"Yes, I am."

"All right. I'll notify them to remove you as a client. Enjoy yourself. Love you. Bye." Charm then clicked off the phone.

"You want me to join you at the château?" Regan asked Garth, speaking into her phone and trying to make sense of what he was saying.

"Yes, my original plans have changed and there's

no need for everything I had set up to go to waste, so I'm asking you."

Regan could only reach one conclusion. For whatever reason, the woman who was supposed to join him was a no-show, and he was inviting her to be with him instead.

Should Regan be upset that she was being asked by default? First of all, she wasn't really a default. He wouldn't expect her to take the woman's place per se. There was no doubt in her mind that he and the woman would have engaged in an affair. That would not be the case for him and Regan. He was merely being kind by inviting her to enjoy some of the things his date was not there to enjoy. Being in his bed would not be one of them.

Knowing how she felt about Garth, could she share space with him and enjoy his company, just like she would if the invitation had come from Jess, Cash, Sloan or Maverick? Garth was her boss; they weren't. As the firstborn, Garth had been groomed to take Bart's place one day, and lately, he hadn't been as approachable as his siblings.

Since becoming his pilot, she could recognize his moods. Although he always exemplified a kind, caring and thoughtful demeanor toward her, she could tell when he was in a more serious state of mind versus a more relaxed one. She was well aware that his disposition was driven by whatever business deals he had on the table. Lately, she'd seen less of his relaxed mood.

She wanted to see more of it.

"Yes, Garth, I'll join you at the château. Thanks for asking."

"I know you wanted to spend a couple of days in LA with your friend. I'll make sure you still get that time on the back end. While you're visiting her, there's a couple of guys I met while stationed there that I can look up. No problem."

"You don't have to do that."

"I don't mind. It's the least I can do to show my gratitude to you for keeping me from getting bored for two weeks. And I recall you mentioning on the flight here that you intended to do some shopping tomorrow. How about if I join you?"

Regan, who'd been about to take a sip of tea, nearly spilled it out of her cup. "You want to go shopping with me?"

"Sure. Why not? It's not like I'm new to the shopping game. Remember I'm Charm's oldest brother, and if Charm's shopping antics haven't driven me crazy, then I'm sure yours won't, either."

"Oh."

"So when do you want me to pick you up from the hotel?"

"I'll be packed and ready to leave whatever time you decide."

"In that case, I'll be there at ten in the morning, Regan."

At exactly ten the next day, Regan watched Garth stride into the hotel's lobby. Her heart skipped and then began to race when he saw her and gave her that Garth Outlaw smile. The one that made her feel all warm inside.

"Good morning, Regan. Are you ready?"

She wasn't sure if she was. She hadn't gotten much sleep last night, wondering if spending two weeks with him was a good idea. Being his pilot was temptation enough. But there was no way she could back out now without him questioning the reason she was doing so.

"Yes, Garth, I'm ready."

"Need help with your luggage?"

"No, I've got this," she said, taking hold of her luggage handle to walk beside him.

"Walker called before I left to come here. Guess what?"

She glanced up at him. "What?"

"The twins were chosen Babies of the Year and will be featured on the cover of some motherhood magazine."

A smile spread across Regan's lips. She'd known Walker Rafferty for as long as she'd known Garth, since the two had been the best of friends from toddlerhood. "That's wonderful."

"I think so, too. Of course, he couldn't wait to tell me since I'm one of the twins' godfathers."

She knew Bailey's oldest brother, Ramsey Westmoreland, was the other godfather. "I haven't seen the twins in a while. I bet they've gotten bigger now," she said.

"They have. I'm happy for Walker. Losing his older son, Connor, was hard on him and he swore he would never have any more children. I'm glad he and Bailey have a beautiful family."

When Garth opened the rental car door for her, he glanced at her and said, "I don't think I've ever heard you say if you plan to settle down, marry and have children, Regan."

She slid onto the seat and snapped her seat belt in place. Pushing her hair back from her face, she said, "Those are my plans one of these days, but I'm in no hurry."

He nodded and then closed the door. Goose bumps formed on her arms as she watched him walk around the front of the car to get in. He had such a sensuous walk. It went well with the rest of him. Today, like her, he was dressed in jeans. The blue polo shirt looked amazing on him and she hoped he thought her blue blouse looked good on her.

"I don't recall sending out the memo," she said.

He glanced over at her as he buckled up. "What memo?"

"The one that told you what colors I was wearing today."

A huge grin spread across his face. "It wouldn't be the first time we've coordinated our outfits without realizing it."

That was true. She'd been his last-minute escort to various functions enough times to know to always pack both semiformal and formal outfits and the necessary accessories.

Before he could start the ignition, she couldn't help but ask, "Why did you want to know about my plans regarding settling down and having children? Dad's been talking to you?"

He shook his head. "No. I asked out of curiosity. Why would you think Franklin has talked to me about that?"

"Because that's all he's been talking about lately.

Now that he's retired and has plenty of free time on his hands, he figures he should be spending it with grand-children he doesn't have yet. He's been dropping hints."

Garth chuckled. "I can see him doing that."

"Dad knows he has to marry me off first. You wouldn't believe how many guys, mainly sons or grand-sons of his new collection of friends from Florida, that he's tried fixing me up with whenever I visit him."

"Annoys you much?"

"Yes, like the dickens," she said grinning. Then, be-cause he'd asked her, she felt it should be okay to ask him. "What about you? Now that Walker has gotten married and become a family man, are you thinking of doing the same?"

Regan had expected a quick yes or no. His hesita-tion gave her pause. "Umm…maybe," he finally said.

Maybe? Now she wondered if his plans to spend two weeks with a woman here in Santa Cruz had been more serious than she thought. All kinds of questions went through her mind. How did the two of them meet? Just how serious were things? If things were serious enough for him to be contemplating settling down, that meant he was finally moving on with his life after los-ing Karen.

"Where do you want to go first?"

She glanced over at him. "I heard that the best shops and markets are located in the Square."

He smiled as he turned on the car's ignition to pull off. "Then that's where we'll go."

Three

An expression of annoyance flitted across Garth's face. If one more man approached Regan to hit on her, he would step in and say something. It didn't matter one iota that she seemed to be doing a good job of handling them herself; it bothered the hell out of him that she had to handle them at all.

He was sitting on a bench on the other side of the store, which provided a good view of her. Unfortunately, other men, too, saw what he saw—a very beautiful woman. But still, that didn't give any man the right to interrupt her shopping.

The man finally moved away and now she was the only one in Garth's line of focus. He studied her striking features. There was her very smooth-looking mocha complexion, a pair of full lips, high cheekbones and almond-shaped, brown bedroom eyes. Her glossy, dark brown hair curled at the ends and hung around her shoulders. And he couldn't dismiss, any more than those other men could, just how good she looked in her jeans and pullover blouse. Regan Fairchild was definitely one delectable package and he wished he hadn't paid attention to that fact.

When a ping alerted him to a notification from his stock app, Garth stood to pull his phone out of the back pocket of his jeans. He smiled seeing the good news that some of his investments were doing extremely well. After putting his phone back in his pocket, he glanced over to where Regan stood and saw yet another man had approached her.

Garth stiffened when he noticed that unlike the other men, she was pretty damn friendly with this particular guy. She was smiling at whatever he was saying. Why?

Deciding it was time to break up that little party, Garth walked toward her, ignoring the little voice telling him she had a right to talk to whomever she wanted, and it wasn't his place to interfere. He ignored that same voice when it accused him of acting territorial.

From the man's accent, which he heard as he came to a stop beside her, Garth guessed this guy was American. "How's the shopping going, Regan?" Garth asked her.

She smiled up at him. "It's going fine. Garth, I'd like you to meet someone," she said, her smile getting even brighter. "This is Lamont Jefferson. Lamont and I attended college together at UCLA."

She turned to the other man. "Lamont, this is my boss, Garth Outlaw."

Garth didn't flinch at the introduction. He wasn't sure why it had bothered him, when technically he *was* her boss. As he and Lamont exchanged handshakes, Garth had a feeling Jefferson was probably wondering why a boss would accompany his employee on a shopping trip.

"What brings you to Santa Cruz?" Garth asked Lamont.

"My wife and I came over on a cruise ship. We split up when I wanted to check out some sporting equipment, and she said she was looking for several new outfits. This was the first ladies' fashion store I came to and figured she'd be in here. While looking around for her, I ran into Regan. Small world."

Regan beamed. "Yes, it is, isn't it?"

Lamont then said, "I'd better check out the other shops for Monica. We'll need to return to the ship in a few hours. It was good seeing you again, Regan, and nice meeting you, Garth."

"Same here," Garth said.

When the man walked out of the store, Garth turned to Regan. "He seems like a nice guy."

"He is. Lamont and I dated for a semester while we attended UCLA."

Raw venom seeped into his gut. He'd gotten that same reaction when Charm had told him about Harold Anders's job offer. Garth had no clue why he would be feeling territorial either time. But then maybe the feeling wasn't territorial but protective. Yes, that had to be it.

"I bet you're getting bored."

Her words intruded into his thoughts. Did she think that was the reason he had come over here? "No, I'm not bored." He glanced down at the outfits slung over her arm. "I see you found several things."

"Yes. I feel like I hit the jackpot. I just have to pay for them and then I'll be ready to go."

He lifted a brow. "Aren't you going to try them on?"

"There's no need. I know my size."

He chuckled. "Charm claims she knows her size, too, but that never stopped her from trying on her clothes. Go ahead. I'll wait. Otherwise, I'm going to feel as if I rushed you."

"Please don't feel that way. I'm sure they'll fit me."

"Humor me anyway, or else I'll think Charm has deliberately taken advantage of my kindness all these years."

She threw her head back and laughed, having no idea how beautiful her neck looked when she did so. "All right, if you're sure. It's your time."

"Yes," he agreed. "It's my time and I have plenty to spare. I'll grab a seat right here to wait."

He watched Regan disappear behind the door that led to the fitting room. While working, she wore her pilot uniform, and on occasion, when she doubled as his chauffeur, she wore a chauffeur uniform. Every so often he saw her dressed formally when she accompanied him to events. He rarely saw her in casual attire, so whenever he did, he couldn't help but appreciate the beautiful woman she was.

In addition to her good looks, Regan had a gorgeous figure, but she'd never been one to flaunt that fact. And he liked it whenever she wore her hair down, where it flowed around her shoulders, which was something she rarely did while working. Usually she wore a ponytail, or had it all stuffed beneath her pilot cap.

As he settled in the chair, he recalled how she'd looked at the Westmoreland Charity Ball, beautiful from head to toe. He released a deep breath, still not certain why that particular night in Denver had been a turning point for him. Not really a turning point but more of an eye-opener. Since then, he'd tried not to be aware of certain things about her, but he'd noticed them anyway. And putting distance between Regan and himself wasn't an option when he'd been flying around the country a lot lately.

He'd meant what he'd told Regan. Going shopping with her was a piece of cake compared to the times he'd gone with Charm. Early on, Bart had declared that one of the brothers would escort Charm whenever she went anywhere, including shopping. She hadn't liked that directive any more than they had.

Instead of taking out her irritation on Bart, she'd unloaded on her brothers and made their shopping trips with her a nightmare. At least for the others, she had. Garth had known how to handle Charm from the beginning, and when she saw that nothing she did rattled him, she soon began behaving. He could honestly say accompanying her on those shopping excursions had turned out to be rather enlightening. She'd told him more than he'd wanted to know about women's undergarments, and how to tell if a woman was wearing any. Charm said she preferred him taking her shopping because he never rushed her out of the stores like Cash, Sloan, Jess and Maverick did. And he never flirted with the sales clerks like Sloan and Maverick. She claimed that Maverick even disappeared a time or two, probably into the ladies' restroom, with a sales clerk. Garth had no reason to doubt her story.

"I'm ready, Garth."

He glanced up and met a smiling Regan. "That was quick."

She chuckled. "While modeling, I learned how to get in and out of my clothes rather quickly."

Why did the image of her doing that very thing suddenly flash in his mind? "I'd forgotten about that time you modeled." Franklin, fearful that his daughter was turning into a tomboy, had enrolled her into etiquette school at sixteen. One of her instructors had persuaded Franklin to let Regan participate in several teen modeling events.

"That was back in the day, but it was fun."

"Do you miss it?" he asked, getting to his feet.

The store clerk had placed all the items she'd purchased in a shopping bag emblazoned with the store's name and logo.

"I didn't do it long enough. Just two years."

He recalled that he and his siblings had attended several of her modeling events. She'd also appeared on the covers of a number of Alaskan teen fashion magazines. After glancing at his watch, he said, "It's a little past noon. I hope you're ready to grab something to eat."

"I am."

"I know how much you like tacos and I overheard

someone mention a place not far from here that sells good ones."

They left the clothing store and headed to the taco shop. "Just so you know, Charm planned this entire trip for me and one of the things she included was a chef who will be at our disposal."

"Sounds nice."

"It is. I met him this morning. And breakfast was delicious."

As they strolled in silence, he was glad they were spending time together like Charm had suggested. The thought that Regan might accept Harold Anders's job offer was bothering him whether he wanted it to or not. The only possible problem he could see in them sharing space for two weeks was his inability to control his attraction to her.

That was basically his problem and not hers.

He credited himself as being a problem-solver and intended to do everything within his power to make sure his desire for her didn't become an issue he couldn't handle.

Regan watched Garth walk into the guest room of the château to place her luggage near the huge bed. Why did he always have to look sexy, no matter what he was wearing or what he was doing? Then there was his scent. Always fresh, robust and manly.

"Thanks for bringing that in, Garth."

"No problem. I hope you find everything satisfactory."

He had to be kidding. The room was gorgeous, and

the view of the mountains outside one window and the sea out the other was spectacular. But then, she could say the same thing about the château itself. It sat high on a hill that overlooked the ocean as well as lush green valleys.

When they'd arrived, she'd been awestruck. The house was a lot bigger than she'd thought, spread out in a way that there were views from every window.

"It's beautiful here, Garth. Thanks for inviting me to stay."

"What time do you want to eat dinner?"

Regan glanced up at him. She hadn't thought they would be sharing all their meals. She'd figured they each would be doing their own thing. "We ate a big lunch, so a late dinner will suit me fine." The tacos had been delicious, and she might have eaten one too many.

"Late is fine with me, too," Garth said. "I'll let you unpack. If you're not too tired in an hour or so, I'd like to give you a tour of the place."

"Okay."

He walked out, leaving her alone. Sighing deeply, she strolled to the window. How many times had she dreamed of this very scenario? To be alone with Garth on some remote island. In her dream it had been a lovers' tryst. One she had hoped for, longed for, for years.

A few minutes later she was unpacking, when her phone rang. She smiled when she saw it was Simone Brinkley, her best friend from college. "Simone, thanks for calling me back."

"No problem. Have you left Santa Cruz and headed my way?"

"There's been a change in plans. I won't be coming to LA just yet. Garth invited me to join him at the château for two weeks," Regan said, placing the phone on speaker so she could talk while putting her clothes away.

"Why would he do that? When we spoke yesterday you suspected he was meeting some woman for a romantic rendezvous."

"I still believe that was the plan, but for some reason, she didn't show up."

"The woman was a no-show and he invited you to stay with him instead?"

Regan began hanging her new outfits in the closet. "It's not like that, Simone. He's my boss."

"A boss you happen to be in love with. How can you do it, Regan?"

She opened one of the dresser drawers to place her lingerie inside. "How can I do what?"

"How can you love Garth the way you do and yet be okay that he only asked you to spend time with him because some woman didn't turn up?"

"Again, Simone, it's not that way. Garth has no idea how I feel about him, and I'm not taking any woman's place. At least not in the way you're insinuating. He doesn't see me that way. To him I'm his employee. He was merely kind enough to invite me to the château to enjoy myself. Not to enjoy him."

"But you love him."

Regan drew in a deep breath. "Yes, but my feelings for Garth are something I have to deal with. Eventually I'll fall out of love with him."

"So far you haven't, and it's been how many years

now, Regan? When we were at UCLA, he was all you ever talked about, and whether you'll admit it or not, I know he's the reason you left LA to return to Fairbanks. Who in their right mind leaves sunny California to go back to icy Alaska?"

Simone was right: Garth was the reason she'd gone back. "It doesn't matter."

"It should matter." Simone paused and then said, "Umm…"

Regan frowned. "What is that 'umm' for?"

"I'm thinking."

Regan knew when it came to Simone, that could be dangerous. As much as she loved her best friend, she refused to let Simone pull her into any shenanigans, and with Simone there could be plenty. As the only child of a single mother, Simone had been raised to believe that she could get anything she wanted if she worked hard and went after it.

"Please don't think, Simone. I've got this."

"No, you don't have this. If you did, you would have Garth Outlaw right where you want him."

"Simone…"

"No, Regan, this might be your only opportunity to go after the one thing you want. The two of you being at the château together is perfect. If I were you, I would seduce the hell out of him. What do you have to lose?"

Regan rolled her eyes. "My job, for one. Are you trying to get me fired?"

"He won't fire you and you know it. You mean too much to him."

"I wish," Regan said, in a whisper.

"Then make it happen, Regan. All it will take is for you to give Garth a hint that you're interested. You're beautiful, smart and intelligent. Who wouldn't want to fall in love with you?"

Regan drew in a deep breath. "You're saying that because you're my best friend."

"No, I honestly believe in your abilities more than you do. You want Garth, and being there with him affords you the perfect opportunity to get him. If you don't go after what you want now, it might be lost to you forever."

Regan shook her head. "I feel sorry for the man you set your sights on. Once you decide he's yours, he won't stand a chance."

The sound of Simone's laughter came through the phone. "Not sure such a man is out there. But if there is, then damn right, I intend to go after him."

Four

Garth stood on the screened-in deck, thinking what a beautiful day it was for mid-October. The weather was perfect, unlike how he knew it would be back home in Fairbanks.

A few minutes ago he had spoken to Jess, who had called to let Garth know he'd returned to Washington. Jess had left Alaska right before what forecasters predicted was the start of the cold season, which was beginning a month earlier than normal.

Garth's gaze moved across the vast amount of land surrounding the château. The view was breathtaking. As far as he could see, there were lush green lands, mountains or ocean. A sense of peace settled over him. It had a lot to do with the view in front of him, and he knew, deep down, it had a lot to do with Regan being here with him.

She hadn't said much while they'd shared lunch, which he'd found odd, since they talked frequently during flights. But he realized they held different conversations then because of their roles. Now they were on equal footing.

He'd finally gotten her to open up by introducing topics they were both familiar with. Like her father and his siblings. He'd enjoyed strolling down memory lane and they'd had quite a few laughs. They'd even talked about Bart and how he still refused to accept the Westmorelands as their kin. By the end of lunch, he'd begun feeling almost that same comfort level he was certain his siblings felt with her.

"I hope I didn't take too long to unpack, Garth."

He turned and immediately felt a sense of déjà vu. Seeing her now renewed the feelings he'd been overpowered by that night at the charity ball. Granted, she wasn't wearing a full-length gown today, but she'd changed out of her jeans and into a long, flowing skirt and billowy blouse. She looked downright sexy; her outfit was a total turn-on.

Instead of answering her question, he asked one of his own, stating the obvious. "You changed clothes?"

She smiled and he felt his gut clench. He knew he had to regain control of his senses or he would lose them totally. "Yes, I decided to wear as many of my new outfits as I could—the ones I bought today, as well as those I brought with me. You like this one?" she asked, twirling around.

He nodded. "Yes, you look nice."

Her smile seemed to brighten. "Thanks. Are you ready to give me a tour of the place?"

"Sure," he said, moving toward her. She had also taken a shower. He knew because her scent of jasmine was even more vibrant.

"We'll start at the front and work our way to the back," he said, leading her to the front door.

"All right."

From there he covered the massive living room and dining area, as well as a spacious eat-in kitchen. There were two sections to the house, east and west. He would be on the east wing and she would be on the west. In the middle was a colossal family room flanked by two Greek pillars. A huge stone fireplace took up one wall. On the opposite wall were floor-to-ceiling windows that overlooked a mountainous waterway. There was also a screened-in patio with a pool and hot tub.

Garth noticed that what had excited her more than anything was the piano that sat in the middle of the living room. He recalled both she and Charm had taken lessons, but Regan had been the one who'd taken those classes seriously. He'd heard her play before and knew she was gifted. He wasn't surprised, since her mother had also been a gifted pianist. It then dawned on him how many things Regan was capable of doing well.

"Thanks again for inviting me to join you."

He smiled over at her. "No problem. It's important to me that you enjoy yourself."

She lifted a brow. "Oh, why?"

There was no way he could tell her what Charm had

shared with him about that job offer from Harold Anders, so he said, "It can't be easy flying me all over the place. And this year has been an extremely busy one. I appreciate all you've done."

What he'd said was true. The company had brought on a number of new clients, which had required flying all over the country for negotiations. Once Bart retired, Garth had begun expanding globally. Sloan was put in charge of international sales and Maverick's job was overseeing the company's expansion into states like Texas, Florida and the Carolinas, for starters. Cash was Garth's right-hand man in the Alaska office, and Charm…well, they were still trying to figure out exactly what her duties were. For now, they involved anything that made her feel useful, and she seemed to be satisfied with that.

And because he didn't want Regan to assume her being here was nothing more than a job perk, he added, "Let me add that my appreciation for you goes beyond your duties to the company, Regan. I would not have issued this sort of invitation to any other employee. I consider our relationship special, mainly because of our family history and friendship. You are someone I trust explicitly."

"Thank you, Garth."

There was a quiet moment between them. Too quiet. He wasn't sure if she felt the sexual chemistry flowing between them, but he certainly did. He felt it to the point he took a step back so he could stay in control and not do anything he would later regret. He checked his watch. "Paulo will be here in a minute."

"Paulo?"

"Yes, he's the chef I told you about. He's on call for the entire two weeks. Because I enjoy cooking, I intend to whip up a few meals for us on my own."

"Like your pancakes?"

Garth chuckled. "Yes, like my pancakes."

During her teen years, when she would spend the weekend with Charm, he had cooked breakfast for everyone. Roberta, who'd been the Outlaws' cook for years, had made use of him in the kitchen when he'd been a kid and gotten underfoot. As a result, he'd discovered that cooking was something he liked, and he had a few signature dishes. After Roberta died, Bart had hired Maddie to take her place, but she wasn't Roberta in the kitchen. So on Maddie's off days Garth had enjoyed feeding his family.

After the tour of the outdoors, they returned to the kitchen to find Paulo had arrived. Introductions were made, and when Regan began speaking to the man in his native tongue, Garth recalled that like him, she was fluent in several languages.

Garth knew Paulo was in his fifties, married, the father of five kids and one grandchild. He had come highly recommended from Garth's cousin Jared Westmoreland. Jared, an attorney living in Atlanta, had brought his wife, Dana, to Santa Cruz last year for their wedding anniversary.

While Paulo was telling them what he would be preparing for dinner, Garth noticed Regan licking her lips. Need sprang to life in the pit of his stomach.

He needed to get a grip.

"I have several activities planned for the next two weeks, but don't let me tire you out. If at any time you prefer doing your own thing, just let me know."

"Okay, I will."

He glanced at a clock on the wall and saw they had a couple of hours before dinner. "I have an idea," he said.

"What?"

"I haven't heard you play piano in years. What do I have to do to get my own private recital?"

She smiled up at him in a way that warmed his insides. "Just ask. I would love to play something for you, Garth."

Regan ended up playing several pieces for him. Each time she finished one and glanced over at him, the look on his face made her insides tingle. It was obvious he liked listening to her play. And she liked looking at him.

Every so often she would find him staring at her. The first time, the sight of him had made her breath catch on a surge of yearning so abrupt it felt like pain. She had to force her fingers to keep moving.

The look had made her wonder if he was thinking of the woman who had not shown up here. How long had he known her? How had they met? She guessed the relationship was serious, since he'd insinuated he was thinking of settling down.

He stood and clapped when her final musical piece came to an end. "That was great, Regan."

"Thanks. That's how I wind down, by playing my piano." He knew about the Steinway Grand piano that she'd bought a couple of years ago.

"I wish Charm had kept up those lessons, but her heart wasn't in them."

She nodded. "No, it wasn't." There was no need to tell him why Charm's heart wasn't in it. At the time, Charm's heart had been into Dylan Emanuel. Dylan, then a seventeen-year-old from Memphis, had won a summer scholarship to attend the University of Alaska's Fairbanks Summer Music Academy. That was where Charm and Dylan had met. One of the instructors teaching Dylan that summer had also been Regan and Charm's piano teacher.

Garth had been away in the military at the time, and when Bart found out about the budding romance, he'd wasted no time putting an end to what he'd called utter teenage nonsense. He thought Charm was too young to consider herself in love with anyone, and that Dylan wouldn't ever amount to anything. Regan wondered if Bart thought that now, since Dylan, with several Grammys under his belt, was being lauded as one of the greatest jazz guitarists of all time.

Regan stood and glanced at her watch. "Goodness, I've been playing for over an hour."

"No problem. Paulo texted to let me know dinner was ready."

"Why didn't you say something? I would have stopped playing."

He smiled. "And that's why I didn't say anything. I didn't want you to stop. I loved hearing you play, and listening to music relaxes me."

She knew that. While in flight he would request all

types of music, but he liked jazz and rhythm and blues the best. "I'll go wash up for dinner."

"Okay, and I'll do the same."

She headed toward the west wing, where her bedroom was located. As tempted as she was, she didn't look back over her shoulder. But why did she have a feeling he was still standing there looking at her?

When she reached her bedroom, she closed the door behind her and leaned against it. As she drew in a deep breath, a low moan escaped her lips. Garth Outlaw had no idea how sexy he looked sitting there with his head thrown back, his long legs stretched out in front of him, his eyes closed while listening to her play.

And then there had been those times when she'd glanced over at him to find him staring at her. Whenever their gazes met, she had fought hard to make her fingers not miss a note. Why had he stared at her that way? What had he been thinking? Maybe he was looking at her, but not thinking about her. Perhaps he'd been thinking of the woman who wasn't here. Longing for her. Wishing Regan was her.

Simone's insinuation that Garth had invited Regan here to take the woman's place came to mind and she pushed it away. She refused to even consider that as a possibility. But what if it was true? She shook her head, refusing to go there. Just like he trusted her, she trusted him.

But she recalled one of her ex-boyfriends once telling her that sex to some men was like an itch. For some, it didn't matter which woman did the scratching.

She was about to go to the bathroom to freshen up

when she heard the sound of voices not far from her bedroom window. She moved toward it, staying back so she couldn't be seen. Garth was outside talking to Paulo, thanking him for preparing dinner and letting him know he would be doing all the cooking tomorrow.

Garth stood and watched Paulo get into his car and leave, but he didn't move to come back inside. Instead, he shoved his hands into the pockets of his jeans and stared out at the long driveway that bordered the beautiful grasslands. He appeared to be deep in thought, and she wondered if he was again thinking about her, the woman who hadn't shown up.

As she continued to watch him, she could no longer deny the intense desire she felt for him. Desire she had no right to feel, but felt anyway. It was the same with the love she'd harbored for years.

Her breath caught when suddenly he looked at her window. She was certain he couldn't see her, but had he detected her presence? The window was open, but she hadn't made a sound. She was sure of that. Yet he stared into the open window as if he was staring straight at her. Like he knew she was staring right back at him. She was conscious of everything about him. It felt like every part of her body was burning inside.

How was she supposed to share dinner with him and keep him from detecting her attraction to him? Granted, she'd done it for years, but this felt different. She was in his space and he was in hers in a way they'd never shared space before. There was no way she could sit across from him at dinner when the mere sight of him made her heart do handsprings in her chest.

She slowly backed away from the window. It was only then that she released a deep breath. A part of her wanted to go tell him she preferred staying at the hotel. But what would she say if he were to ask why?

Regan knew she had to make it through these two weeks without giving anything away. After that, it would be business as usual. He would be her boss and she would be his pilot, and nothing more.

Five

Garth knew the moment Regan had moved away from the window. He hadn't seen her, but he had known she was there. Her scent had given her away. He had looked toward the window, yet she hadn't said or done anything to give away her presence. Why? Why had she stayed hidden from him?

He remembered when she'd glanced up and caught him staring at her while she played the piano. Instead of looking away, she'd held his gaze while she continued playing. Intense heat had curled his insides as their gazes connected, held, locked. On top of that, he'd felt his body's most primal urges kick in, reminding him just how long he'd been without a woman. Too long.

He could blame his celibacy on his workload, but he knew it was more than that. Even the woman from the dating agency, although attractive in the photos and meeting all his specifications, wasn't the woman he dreamed about when he went to sleep at night. The woman he longed to make love to. The woman who'd become his fantasy girl.

That woman was Regan.

Just thinking about how much he desired her had a hard hum of lust rushing through his veins.

There was no way she hadn't felt something, as well. He'd known the exact moment her nipples had hardened into buds and pressed against her blouse. And the pulse in her throat had thumped erratically, a clear indication she wasn't immune to what was taking place between them.

And something *was* taking place, and not just on his end.

The question he needed to ask was whether or not this attraction between them was something he wanted to incite. If so, why? And if not, then why not? There was no way he would let her go work for another company without putting up a fight. She was a vital asset to his company—someone he depended on, someone he trusted. Then, on a more personal note, she was someone who stirred his insides and fired up his desire without even trying. No other woman had done that since Karen. And there wasn't a damn thing he could do about it.

Why was he even trying?

He knew one good reason without even thinking about it. *Franklin.*

Regan's father meant the world to him. Garth admired the man and highly respected him. In some ways, he had a closer relationship with Franklin than with his own father. Bart had been hard to deal with at times. He still was. But Franklin had always been Franklin. He'd been the one Garth had gone to for advice or when he needed an ear during those times he'd had to take on Bart.

Franklin had always been the voice of reason. The one who seemed to understand Bart to the point where he'd begged his sons to try to understand him, as well. Garth was certain Franklin was privy to secrets regarding Bart that Franklin wouldn't divulge. Like the reason Bart refused to acknowledge his relationship with the Westmorelands.

"I'm back."

He glanced up and released a deep moan, hoping Regan hadn't heard it. She was wearing the same outfit and her hairstyle was the same. So why had he gotten such a gut reaction upon seeing her again? That didn't make sense.

"I was hoping I had time to set the table before you returned," he said, trying to figure out why his attraction to her was more intense at this moment than ever before.

"Since I'm here, I can help you."

Her help was the last thing he wanted because that would put her too close for comfort. However, there was no way he could turn down her offer. "Thanks. I'd appreciate it."

"Do you think I can kidnap Paulo and get away with it?"

Garth grinned. "You want to kidnap Paulo?"

"Why not?" Regan asked, licking her lips.

Garth fought the heat curling in his gut every time Regan did that with her mouth. Watching her eat was arousing. She would do well to keep her tongue inside her mouth. Every time she licked her lips he was tempted to show her the proper way it was done. On further thought, it would be the improper way. Definitely indecent. Why did indecent appeal to him?

"For starters," he said, shifting slightly in his chair to relieve the tightness in his crotch, "there is the matter of a wife, five kids and a grandchild."

She lifted what he thought was a cute brow. "Do you think they could be bribed?"

He grinned again. "Possibly. But wouldn't it be less of a criminal offense and a hell of a lot cheaper if you ask him for the recipe?"

She pretended to give his suggestion serious thought. "Only problem is that I don't follow a recipe worth a damn, Garth. You of all people should know that."

Yes, he should. He recalled that time years ago when she'd been fourteen or fifteen and had gotten a recipe from him to prepare her father a batch of cookies. Franklin had nearly broken his tooth when he'd bitten into one. He'd told Garth—behind Regan's back of course—that he would use the things for target practice.

"That was years ago," he said. "I would hope you've gotten better."

She chuckled. "Nope. I hate to disappoint you."

"You could never disappoint me, Regan." Although she might not be the greatest cook, she definitely had other talents—like playing piano, speaking several languages, walking with perfect posture and flying a plane.

He pushed his plate aside, inwardly admitting his cousin Jared hadn't lied. Paulo was the best. Garth had eaten other veal dishes, but nothing like the one he'd eaten tonight. Paulo had roasted the veal with potatoes in some special sauce. The same sauce that had Regan licking her lips.

He had to stop himself from licking his own lips.

He glanced back at Regan. She was licking her lips again and looking blatantly sexy while doing it. She gazed over at him and smiled. "Now for the dessert."

The dessert Paulo had made looked delicious, but the man sitting across the table from her looked delectable. Regan leaned back in her chair and smiled. Sharing both lunch and dinner with Garth had brought back pleasant childhood memories, reminding her of how much they'd been a part of each other's lives.

She recalled Bart always being distant, at least until Charm arrived. And she knew he wasn't the easiest person to get along with. He and his sons had clashed a number of times. Regan had once asked her father how he could work for a man who at times seemed so detached. Her father had simply said he understood Bart. There were things that had happened in Bart's life that he was still trying to work through. Her father never said what those things were and he would not have said, even if she'd asked.

Regardless of Bart's moody ways, because of her friendship with the Outlaws, she'd had a fun childhood. But that didn't mean there hadn't been periods of loneliness as the brothers got older and before Charm arrived. Being an only child had been tough, especially during those times when her father traveled a lot. But whenever he came home, Franklin Fairchild made sure she'd known just how much she was loved and wanted.

"Which one of these you want to try first?"

A smile spread across her lips when Garth held up the platter of delicious-looking treats. "Um, I think I'll try that strawberry twist," she said, leaning up to get it off the platter.

When Garth's gaze dipped to her chest, she realized how much of her cleavage he was seeing. She quickly sat back down. "Ah, could you pass the tray to me?"

"Certainly." Instead of passing it, he stood and walked it over to her.

Regan's heart thudded while watching him. "Thanks."

"You're welcome. Anything else you want while I'm up?"

She nervously shook her head. "No. That's all."

She then studied him as he returned to his seat, appreciating every step. He had such a nice backside. Could she fault him for taking a peek down her blouse when she was definitely drooling over his rear end?

"I think an evening walk is in order."

She blinked. "Excuse me?"

He smiled. "After all we've eaten today, I think we need to walk off the calories."

Regan took a sip of her wine. "Taking a walk sounds like a good idea."

She bit into her pastry and glanced over to see his eyes were on her. Specifically, her mouth. "Is something wrong, Garth?"

"No. Is it good?"

She smiled as she licked a crumb that clung to her lower lip. "Very much so. You ought to try one."

"I might later."

Regan noticed he was still staring at her while she ate her pastry. What he was thinking? Could Simone have been right? Was he attracted to her, even a little? "Are you sure you want me to take a walk with you?"

His gaze held hers when he said, "I'm positive. Why wouldn't I?"

"Don't you remember what happened the last time we took a walk together?"

He didn't say anything for a moment and then a smile spread across his face. "Oh, yes. That was the time you were to keep me occupied while Charm tried sneaking that cat with all her kittens into the house. You pretended you needed to interview someone for one of your classes."

She grinned. "I *did* have to interview someone for one of my classes. I didn't lie about that."

"Whatever you say."

She tilted her head to look at him, unable to hide her smile. "Why do I get the feeling you don't believe me?"

He smiled at her. "Because I don't. So, eat all the sweets you want so we can take that walk."

Six

After Garth and Regan changed their shoes, they left the château. They'd seen a trail earlier and intended to find out where it led. It had been a gorgeous day that turned into a beautiful evening. Although the sun had gone down and the winds coming off the ocean were brisk, she was enjoying the mild temperature.

At first they walked side by side, not saying much. Then he started off the conversation as they continued walking down the path. "Are you missing Fairbanks?"

She glanced over at him. "Not really. The only thing I look forward to this time of year is the first snowfall and the northern lights. They're beautiful."

"Yes, they are," he agreed.

It felt odd taking the time to give a woman his undivided attention. Bottom line, he was enjoying Regan's company in spite of one unnerving problem: being around her was stirring his libido like crazy. Like now. And at dinner, when she'd caught him staring down her blouse.

Instead of talking about work, he discussed Maverick's latest escapades. She had known the family long enough to know that of all his brothers, Maverick always managed to live up to his name. He liked thinking outside the box. Maverick was the one Garth could count on to come up with innovative ideas.

Although she laughed, not surprisingly, in the end she came to Maverick's defense. Since he was closer to her in age than the other brothers, Regan and Maverick had spent more time together and had always gotten on well together.

They talked about worldwide events and music and the books she'd read. And he tried to keep his concentration on their discussion while studying the beauty of her eyes, the texture of her skin and the shape of her lips.

When he fell silent, she shifted the conversation again. "I like your cousins, the Westmorelands. I especially liked talking to Ian. It seems the two of you have a lot in common."

He knew what she was referring to. Although Ian owned a casino in Lake Tahoe, he was also big on astronomy like Garth. Ian had graduated from Yale University magna cum laude, with a degree in physics. After graduation he'd worked at NASA's Goddard Space Flight Center. Although he no longer worked there, he hadn't given up his love of astronomy.

Garth's own fascination with science had begun with the northern lights. He'd kept up the interest through high school, at the University of Alaska in Juneau and into the Marines. His degree was in Transportation and Logistics with a minor in Physics and Astronomy.

"Yes, Ian is a swell guy. It would have been nice to have known him years ago. Then I wouldn't have felt like the only geek in the family."

"You weren't a geek."

He shrugged. "For a while Bart thought so." And that was putting it mildly.

Bart had been disappointed to discover transportation wasn't foremost in his oldest son's mind when he'd left for college. Although Garth knew he would work for the company, he'd seen nothing wrong with getting a minor in a subject he loved.

He decided to ask Regan something he was more than mildly curious about. "Are you still seeing Craig Foster?"

She slowed her pace. "How did you know I was dating Craig?" she asked while pushing a lock of hair back from her face.

"Franklin mentioned him. Maverick and Sloan did, as well."

She nodded. "And I guess Dad also mentioned that he didn't like him."

"Yes, he did say something to that effect."

She shrugged. "There was nothing wrong with Craig other than that he was military. Dad never cared for me dating a military man for fear I would end up marrying one and moving away."

"Yes, there was always that possibility. I'm sure you would have moved to wherever your husband got stationed, right?"

"No. I would never have left Dad."

He wondered if that was her way of saying those military guys she'd dated were not serious involvements. "You would not have?"

"Nope. But then Dad left me."

Just like she'd come to Maverick's defense, he came to Franklin's. "The cold weather was getting to be too much for him, Regan. Surely you understood that."

"Yes, I understood it, Garth. But the decision to move to Florida happened so unexpectedly. I dropped by one day and he told me his mind was made up."

He smiled. "You know as well as I do that Franklin has never been one to procrastinate about anything." Then, to get back to his earlier question, he asked, "So, what's the deal with you and Craig Foster?"

She sighed. "Craig and I aren't seeing each other anymore. It was a mutual decision to go our separate ways."

"I see." He couldn't help wondering why. She was right about Franklin not liking the guy. But not for the reason Regan assumed. Franklin was a good judge of character and sensed Foster was the overly jealous type. Garth hadn't met Foster, but Maverick and Sloan had. Not surprisingly, they hadn't liked him, either.

"So, what's the deal with you and the woman you were to meet here for two weeks?"

Garth figured she had every right to ask, since he had inquired into her business. "We've known each other for a couple of months and decided to get together here. Something came up at the last minute and she couldn't make it."

That wasn't totally true, but it hadn't been an outright lie, either. The dating service had provided him with details a couple of months ago and the mix-up in dates had been discovered at the last minute. He figured there was no need to tell Regan they'd met through a dating service.

"What are your plans for tomorrow?"

He glanced over at her and hoped his plans were her plans. He would make sure of it.

"We have a private tour of the island scheduled for tomorrow."

"A private tour?"

"Yes. The driver will pick us up and bring us back afterward. It's a four-hour tour with a number of interesting places for us to see."

They had come to the end of the walking path at a cliff overlooking the sea. "This place is beautiful," she said. "I bet it's beautiful at night, too."

He bet it was. He could just imagine how the stars would look over the ocean. "Ready to head back?"

A smile touched the corners of her lips and his breath suddenly caught on a surge of yearning.

"Yes, I'm ready to head back."

"What time do we leave for the tour tomorrow morning?" Regan asked when they returned to the château.

He glanced over at her as he closed the door behind them. "If we leave here by ten, we should be fine. And I plan to prepare breakfast before we leave."

"Pancakes?"

He chuckled. "Yes, pancakes. I suggest you get up by eight."

"Need help?"

A grin touched his lips. "You know better. Cooking is therapy for me. I like doing it myself."

She saw he was leaning against one of the gigantic pillars. It was one sexy pose, and for a minute she envisioned him as a Greek god. "I was just thinking how when we were kids, you liked cooking for us. We got to play cards or board games while we waited. You guys had a lot of them."

He chuckled. "And if I recall, Scrabble was your favorite."

She was surprised he remembered. "Yes, I loved Scrabble."

"You would challenge Sloan because the words he came up with were never real words."

"Yes, and he figured I was too dumb to figure it out," she said, laughing. "He was so arrogant."

Garth joined in her laughter. "Was? He still is."

Her shoulders shook again in laughter. "I have to admit, playing that game definitely enhanced my vocabulary."

"That was the plan."

Regan sighed deeply. "You were always the mature one. Very responsible. Looking out for everyone. Taking care of us, with Walker's help of course."

He grinned. "Of course. I was the oldest and Walker was my sidekick. Someone had to keep you guys out of trouble."

"And then you and Walker left for college."

He nodded. "Yes, however, we didn't go far and came home practically every weekend."

But still, she thought, it hadn't been the same. Things had gotten interesting when Charm had arrived. By then, Garth and Walker had returned home for a year before going into the military. That was all the time needed for Garth to take a firm hand to Charm, then leaving it to his brothers to do the rest when it became apparent Bart wouldn't.

"I think I'll go take a shower now," Garth said.

"I'll take one, too, and get into bed early to make sure I'm up at eight."

"I'm sure all that shopping wore you out," Garth said, chuckling.

"For your information, it was the walk that did it. I'm not into a lot of physical activity."

"Well, that's going to change while you're here, because I *am* into physical activities. I suggest we take a walk every evening."

The expression on his face was serious. "I'll think about it," she said, grinning.

"Yes, you do that."

She would—and there were other things she would think about. Like should she consider Simone's advice. Simone hadn't been the only person who'd suggested Regan catch Garth's eye. Charm had suggested that same thing, but that had been years ago. Charm probably figured Regan had gotten over her crush on Garth by now. If Charm thought that, then she was partly right. It was no longer a crush.

Now it was a lot more than that.

"I'll see you in the morning, Regan."

"Okay, Garth. Good night."

She'd started moving toward her bedroom when he called out to her. "Regan?"

She stopped to turn around. He was still leaning against the pillar and looking so sexy that a deep hunger, one she'd never felt before, invaded her midsection. "Yes?"

"Pleasant dreams."

She swallowed and forced herself to speak. "Pleasant dreams to you, too."

She turned back around and stepped away, walking as quickly as her legs would carry her.

Garth stood there long after Regan closed her bedroom door. Was he wrong to fight this inner turmoil he felt whenever he was around her? Did it make sense to place distance between them? That would be hard to do since they were here together.

They'd again taken a stroll down memory lane, and the one thing he *could* accept was that Regan wasn't a kid anymore. She had stopped being a kid long ago. Now that he'd finally noticed, was it wrong to want to do something about it?

He rubbed his hand down his face. Had she felt the desire radiating within him? Had she detected his need, his passion, his wants? His attraction? It was an attraction he had controlled since last year.

How long could he continue to control it? Why was he even trying?

He pushed away from the pillar and moved toward his bedroom. He needed to take a shower and he intended for it to be a damn cold one.

Seven

The aroma of strawberry pancakes had Regan opening her eyes with a huge smile on her face. Shifting her body in bed, she glanced at the clock on the nightstand to make sure she hadn't overslept. In fact, she still had thirty minutes to spare.

She had gone to bed early last night, not because she was tired but because if she'd spent just one more minute in Garth's presence, she would have given away her true feelings for him. That was why she was glad he hadn't pressed her for more information regarding her breakup with Craig.

The last thing she wanted him to know was that the reason she and Craig broke up was that he'd accused her of having an affair with Garth. And all because one of his friends in Denver had texted Craig the link to an article about the Westmoreland Charity Ball. Just so happened the article included a photo of her and Garth dancing together. Craig believed she wasn't sleeping with him because she was sleeping with Garth. That was when she'd told him to leave and not show his face again. She was glad she hadn't heard from him since.

Refusing to think about Craig any longer, she got out of bed, showered and dressed. In no time at all, she was walking to the kitchen. The closer she got, the more she picked up the smell of coffee brewing and bacon frying.

"Good morning, Garth," she greeted, sliding onto a stool at the breakfast bar.

Garth turned around and smiled at her. This smile wasn't any different than the others he'd always given her, but for some reason this one made her feel special. He looked good dressed in a pair of khakis and a green polo shirt. She'd always thought the color green enhanced his features. And she might be mistaken, but his eyes appeared darker than usual.

"Good morning, Regan."

She smiled back and for just a heartbeat, their gazes held. He turned back to the stove, but she was certain she hadn't imagined it.

"I hope you slept well," he tossed over his shoulder.

"I did. Thanks."

She studied his body, and the woman in her appreciated how his slacks stretched across his well-rounded backside and tapered down a pair of muscular thighs. Why did it suddenly feel so hot? And why was her heart pounding? Clearing her throat, she asked, "Need help with anything?"

"You can set the table for me. I figure it would be nice to sit in the dining room and take advantage of the view."

"Yes, that would be nice," she agreed, sliding off the stool.

She leaned up to get a couple of plates out of the cabinet at the same time he turned to place a plate of bacon on the counter. They nearly collided.

"Oops. Sorry," he said.

"No problem." Moving out of his way, she got the plates. Yesterday, the kitchen had seemed huge. Why, with both her and Garth in it, was it as if it had shrunk? Going to the drawer for the silverware, she was tempted to glance over her shoulder at him, but she resisted.

"Glad you woke up on your own. I wondered if I would have to wake you."

Now she did turn to look at him. Was he serious or just joking? She could just imagine him coming into her bedroom to wake her. Then, no, she couldn't imagine it. She didn't *want* to imagine it. Doing so would play havoc on her hormones. From the mischievous look that appeared in his eyes, she figured he was just joking.

"You would not have had to wake me. I have a built-in alarm clock. Got it from Dad."

"Yesterday, I noticed something else you got from your dad."

"Oh, what?"

"Your ability to add stuff up in your head. You did it yesterday at the restaurant. It always amazed me how Franklin could do that. As a kid I struggled with math and he would give me pointers, or shortcuts as he would call them."

Yes, that was another gift she had inherited from her father. Because her mother had died when she was young, she didn't remember much about her. However, she knew how much she looked like her, because her father had kept pictures around the house.

"You okay over there?"

She closed the utensils drawer and glanced over at him. "Yes, I'm fine. I was just thinking of my mom."

"At least you have one to think about."

She met his gaze. There hadn't been any bitterness in his tone. The words had been spoken matter-of-factly. She'd been around the Outlaw brothers enough to know the subject of their mothers was a joke to them. Garth had written off his mother years ago when she had left him with Bart and then remarried. She'd had other children, but none of them had ever reached out to Garth. His mother hadn't, either.

"Do you ever hear from her, Garth?"

He would have every right to tell her it was none of her business, but he didn't. Instead, he said, "No. I understand her other son just finished law school and her daughter is in med school."

She wanted to ask where he'd obtained that information, but she didn't press her luck. Evidently, he read her mind.

"I looked her up once, right before I left for the military. I called to see if she would meet with me. At first, she said no, but then she agreed. I invited her to dinner, and she had pictures of her family. I asked if I could meet them, and she said she preferred I didn't. I was a part of her life she didn't want to remember. I suggested she let her son and daughter decide, and she said they had. They knew about me and didn't want to meet."

"You believe that?"

"No reason not to. Doesn't matter. I left satisfied that I had reached out to her. If she and her family didn't want me to be a part of their lives, then so be it."

She nodded. It was his decision to make. Moving out of the kitchen, she went into the dining room to set the table. He followed, carrying several platters.

"It's just the two of us. How do you think we'll eat all that food?" she asked him.

He shrugged. "It's not really a lot, and between the two of us none of it will go to waste, trust me."

"If you say so." She knew he was a hearty eater and figured the reason he kept in great shape was because he had a workout room in his basement and he stayed active.

Breakfast was enjoyable, and the pancakes were delicious. He told her of the places the private tour would take them and figured they should be back before two. What really sounded good was his offer to grill hamburgers for lunch.

"I talked to Maverick and Sloan last night," he said as they cleared the table. "I mentioned you were here with me and they threatened me bodily harm if I didn't make sure you had a good time."

After they'd loaded the dishes into the dishwasher, she glanced at her watch. "We've made good time. I'll be ready to leave once I change shoes."

"All right."

Regan walked off, and although she didn't look back, she again had a feeling Garth was watching her.

"Need help?" Garth asked, moving to assist Regan with her packages as they entered the château. It seemed every stop they made on the sightseeing tour, she had run into a shop to purchase souvenirs. She'd made a list that he knew included his brothers, Charm, her father and Bart, as well as some of her friends.

"Yes, thanks."

She passed one of the bigger bags to him. He got close enough to inhale her scent. He'd smelled jasmine on other women, but for some reason the scent was different on her.

"You're still grilling hamburgers?"

He glanced over at her. "Yes. You're hungry?"

She scrunched up her face. "I wasn't going to say anything, but with all that walking we did, breakfast has worn off."

"Then I'll get started right away. I've even thought about getting in the pool."

"Now that's something you wouldn't be doing this time of year in Alaska," she said.

"True," he said, placing the bag on the table. "You want to join me for a swim?"

Regan turned and lifted a brow. "You want me to go swimming with you?"

She seemed surprised that he'd asked. "Yes."

She smiled. "I'm glad one of the things I bought that day we went shopping was a swimsuit."

"That's good."

He had enjoyed her company again today. Her excitement had been contagious. Their tour guide had been thorough and full of historical facts, and Regan had asked a lot of questions.

Garth watched as she grabbed her bags and walked toward her bedroom. He rubbed his hands down his face. She was sexiness on legs. He'd never seen a walk so graceful be such a turn-on. Before closing her bedroom door, she glanced over her shoulder and saw him still standing there, staring.

A confused frown settled on her face. "Is anything wrong, Garth?"

For a quick second, he was tempted to give her a straight answer, to tell her that yes, something was wrong. He'd come here to meet a woman who was supposed to help him control his intense attraction to Regan. Because of a mix-up, the woman was a no-show, and now the very object of his desire was under the same roof, breathing the same air, sharing his space and blowing his mind every time she walked or talked.

Instead, he said, "No, nothing is wrong. I was just thinking about something."

"Oh. Okay." She closed the bedroom door.

It was only then that he turned to go to his own room.

Garth was already on the patio seasoning the burgers when Regan joined him. Although she wore a cover-up over her bathing suit, he could clearly see the outlines of a very shapely figure. He tried keeping his attention on the meat.

"You can go ahead and get in the pool if you want. I want to get the meat on the grill."

"Need help?"

He appreciated how she always offered. "No, I've got this. Thanks for asking."

Garth then turned his attention back to the grill. He heard her moving behind him, sliding off her sandals. Out of his peripheral vision, he saw her take off her cover-up. Every nerve in his body hummed with lust.

He was so consumed by his physical reaction that the loud sound of her splash made him jump. Deciding that he couldn't resist temptation any longer, he glanced at her in the pool and wasn't surprised that she was a good swimmer. Regan was good at so many things.

Garth turned his attention back to the grill. When he was satisfied it would be a while before the hamburgers needed him again, he left the patio and went into the kitchen to make a salad and fries. It was too early to start on the fries, but he could certainly get the salad into the refrigerator. He was almost done when he looked out the French door—at the exact moment Regan eased out of the water.

He nearly dropped the bowl while watching water pour off her skin. But what really held his attention was her bathing suit. It was a one piece, but for all he cared, it could have been a no-piece. It clung to her skin like a second layer. The shape and cut were perfect for every single contour of her body. He tore his gaze off her to quickly finish the salad, anxious to join her in the pool.

"I hope you're not through with your swim," he said,

returning to the patio to find her stretched out on one of the loungers.

"No, I decided to take a break."

"I hope it's not a long one. I want to swim a few laps with you, after I take the meat off the grill."

Garth was a sharp businessman because he could read people. It bothered him that he saw apprehension in her expression now, which led him to say, "But only if you don't mind."

She met his gaze. "No, I don't mind."

It didn't take him long to finish the hamburgers and place them in the warmer. He walked toward where she lay on the lounger while flipping through a magazine. She had put her cover-up back on. Why? Was she nervous about him seeing her in a bathing suit that looked damn good on her?

Upon hearing his approach, she looked up. "Are you ready for me, Garth?"

Her words, innocently spoken, stirred something deep within him. It was a part of his body that just didn't want to behave around her. Regan was off-limits. When he returned to Alaska, he would call one of his female acquaintances to take care of his manly needs. But even as he had the thought, he said, "Yes, Regan, I am ready for you."

Eight

Regan watched Garth ease out of his jeans, and sensations she'd never felt before passed through her.

His swimming trunks looked good on him, fitting perfectly on his masculine thighs. Even in his business suits he could start her heart fluttering.

"I'll be back. I want to grab a couple more towels."

She watched him sprint off, feeling her heart against her ribs. Moving quickly toward the pool, she decided to be in the water when he returned. She was somewhat nervous at the thought of Garth seeing her in a bathing suit.

"You're in the water already."

Not only was she in the water, she was submerged in the deep end. Was that disappointment she heard in his voice? "Yes, I decided to go ahead and get in."

He jumped in, making a big splash. Her heart began beating fast as she watched him move agilely through the water, using a perfectly executed breaststroke.

"You want to do a few laps together?" he asked when they were less than a few feet apart.

"Sure."

"You have a nice bathing suit, by the way."

"Thanks. Ready for those laps?"

He nodded. "We are not competing, Regan. We're doing laps together. I felt I needed to say that just in case you're like Charm, who has a bunch of competitive genes in her body."

Regan tilted her head, chuckling. "I promise not to tell her you said that."

"Please don't. I have enough to deal with as it is, when it comes to Charm."

She could hear the brotherly fondness in his voice. Any other family that consisted of six siblings, all of whom had different mothers, would certainly be dysfunctional to the nth degree. But not the Outlaws.

"Ready to start?" Garth asked her.

"Yes, I'm ready."

Their bodies moved in sync as they glided through the water. The pool was large enough that they had their own space, yet their moves felt choreographed. As if on cue, when they reached the other side, they turned to go back to the other side of the pool.

They did a number of laps before she eased over to the side of the pool. She wanted to watch him work his body.

"You're leaving me?" he asked, treading water as he watched her.

"For the time being. I don't have as much stamina as you do."

When she was on the other side of the pool, he began swimming. His body maneuvered several different strokes masterfully, and he looked amazing while gliding through the water.

Regan lost track of time. Maverick was right about Garth having a lot of stamina. She couldn't help but be curious whether he took that same level of vigor to the bedroom. She wasn't shocked to be wondering such a thing since she had long ago accepted Garth as a fantasy lover.

"Daydreaming?"

Regan sucked in a deep breath. She hadn't known he'd come to join her at the side of the pool. "Excuse me?"

A smile touched the corners of his lips. "I asked if you were daydreaming. You looked as if your thoughts were a million miles away."

Regan wondered what he would think if he knew her thoughts had been right here in the pool with him. "I was just deciding it's time to get something to eat."

He nodded. "Everything is ready but the French fries and that won't take but a few minutes in the air fryer."

"Okay." She just realized how close they were standing. She was tempted to reach out and rub her hands down his wet chest. But she wouldn't stop there. Then she would lean in and lick the side of his neck, and then...

"Did I tell you how nice you look in your bathing suit?"

"Yes, you did. Thanks."

"I got an idea of what we can do after we eat, if you aren't tired."

She licked her lips. "What?"

"Something we haven't done in a long time."

Her thoughts were on making love, but she figured that wasn't it, since they'd never done that before at all. "What?"

"Play Scrabble."

She couldn't help but smile. It had been years since she'd played. "Um, why do I get the feeling that I'm about to find out that Charm and Maverick aren't the only Outlaws with competitive genes?"

"What! You're challenging me again, Regan?" Garth said, grinning broadly.

"You bet I am. *Lionize* is not a word."

"Yes, it is." He didn't want to argue with her, but darn, she looked so cute when she was angry. Especially the way her lips formed into a pout. He took a sip of his wine, needing something to soothe the sensations rolling around too close to his groin.

"Then prove it."

"You do realize, Regan, that you can't afford to challenge me again, right?"

She lifted her chin. "Is that what you're counting on? That I'll let you get away with this one?"

"No.

"Then I'm challenging you, Garth. Prove it."

"Okay." He picked up his phone.

"No, this time, we are using mine," she said, standing to pull her cell phone out of the back pocket of the denim shorts she had changed into after their swim. He thought now what he always thought whenever he saw her legs. She had a gorgeous pair.

"Are you accusing me of cheating?" he asked, amused when he probably should feel offended.

"I'm not accusing you of anything. I'd just rather use my phone to look it up this time."

He shrugged. "Fine, go right ahead. And just so you know, you're cute when you're mad."

She frowned. "I'm not mad."

"If you aren't, then you could have fooled me. You know what I think?"

"No, what do you think?"

"I think you've been hanging around Maverick and Charm too long."

"Whatever," she said, rolling her eyes, as she pulled up the dictionary on her cell phone.

Garth watched her expression and knew the exact moment she saw challenging him had been a mistake. He couldn't resist adding salt to the wound by saying. "So, what does it say? What's the definition?"

"It doesn't matter," she said, placing her phone aside and picking up her wineglass.

"It matters to me. So, what does it say?"

Her annoyance was apparent when she picked up her phone and read aloud what it said. "To *lionize* is to treat someone as a celebrity." She looked back over at him. "Happy now?"

He leaned back in his chair and smiled over at her. Yes, he was happy. He had spent all day with her and tomorrow he would be doing the same—as well as the day after, and the day after that. He had twelve more days to be with her and he was looking forward to each of them. Around her, he felt relaxed. At least he did whenever he wasn't lusting after her.

"Yes, I'm happy, but I want you to be happy, too, Regan. So, I guess that means I'm going to have to start *lionizing* you."

A smile broke out on her pouty lips. Shaking her head, she said, "You just couldn't resist, could you?"

He chuckled, moving the board game aside to put it away. "Enough of Scrabble. The last thing I want is for you to walk around mad with me for the next two weeks."

"I couldn't ever get mad at you, Garth."

He glanced over at her. Instead of meeting his gaze, she was taking a sip of her wine while looking at the fireplace he'd lit earlier. Paulo had warned him that this time of year, Santa Cruz had warm days and cool nights. Since the château was right off the ocean, the evening temperature would drop rather quickly. They found his warning to be true. No sooner had they gotten out of the pool and eaten than the temperature fell. They were surprised, since it hadn't done so last night when they'd taken a walk.

"Besides," she said, finally looking at him. "I can't get mad at you since you're my boss and I need my job."

He took another sip of his wine. For some reason, it was important that while they were there together, their employer-employee relationship didn't exist. He wanted her to feel comfortable with him.

"That might be true, but while we're here together, we don't have a professional relationship. I invited you to stay here and to share my space not as my pilot, but as a friend. The person I cooked breakfast for this morning, went on a tour with today, went swimming with and beat at Scrabble, is someone I consider a friend."

A huge smile touched her lips. "There you go, rubbing salt into the wound again."

He laughed. "It's not intentional." He became silent for a moment and then said in a more somber tone, "But seriously, you understand what I'm saying, right? I don't want you to think I would invite other female employees to spend time with me this way. I feel comfortable with you and with being alone here with you. And I hope the same holds true for you."

She nodded, a serious expression appearing on her face, as well. "Yes, of course.

"Good. Do you have any questions or concerns you think we should address?"

She hesitated but then said, "Yes, there is one thing that's concerning for me."

"And what is it?"

Garth watched Regan nibble on her bottom lip. He'd known her long enough to know that whatever this concern was, she was nervous about bringing it up.

"You can talk to me about anything, Regan. That hasn't changed."

She met his gaze. "What about her? The woman you were supposed to spend time with here, who didn't

come? There are some women who wouldn't appreciate their man spending two weeks with another woman,
no matter how innocent the relationship. What if she
doesn't understand the kind of friendship we share and
thinks us being here means more than it does? Will she
understand our unique relationship?"

Their unique relationship...

He'd never thought of their relationship as such, but
that was definitely one way to define it. For her to ask
such a question showed the depth of her concern. And
from her standpoint he understood why she would be
concerned. But that was only because she didn't know
the truth.

Although he wouldn't share any details about the
dating service or his plans to settle down, he could certainly address her concerns. "Don't worry about her,
Regan."

He could tell from the look on her face that those
words hadn't waylaid her concerns. "Why not?"

He met her gaze and held it. "Because you don't have
to. You're going to have to trust me on this."

Regan looked into his eyes, considering his words.
Maybe the relationship with the woman who hadn't arrived wasn't as serious as she'd assumed. Even then, it
wasn't like Garth to spend two weeks anywhere with
a woman if it wasn't serious. Other men might do such
a thing, but not Garth.

Knowing he was waiting for some kind of response,
she said, "Then I guess that settles it, because I do trust
you."

Looking at her watch, she decided it was time to retire for the night. "I need to call Simone to tell her about my change in plans." Simone already knew, but Garth didn't have to know that. At the moment Regan just needed to escape from his presence. There was only so much of him she could take. His entire aura was overpowering.

"Okay. Paulo will be back tomorrow. If you want breakfast, he will be here by nine. I plan to go sailing. You can join me if you like."

She would definitely like, but she didn't want to crowd him. They had spent today together, and it might be a good idea to have space for both of them tomorrow. "Thanks, but I brought a book to read. One written by your cousin Rock Mason. It's good." Rock Mason was the pen name of his cousin Stone Westmoreland.

"I heard his books are good. I haven't had time to read one. By the way, according to our agenda, we're to attend the opera tomorrow night. It's a dressy affair."

She'd forgotten all about that. When he'd shown her the itinerary a couple of days ago, she'd been excited at the idea of going. She'd brought a gown that would be perfect. At the time, she'd packed it just in case she and Simone decided to do something fancy while she was in Los Angeles.

"I'm good with dressy and would love to go. It doesn't start until eight, so I'll be well rested by then, but the question of the hour is whether or not you'll be rested, since you're going sailing tomorrow, Garth."

"I should be fine, so let's plan to go."

"Okay. Good night, Garth."

"Good night, Regan. Sleep well."

Later that night, when Regan slid between the sheets with her e-reader in her hand, she couldn't help but think about how much she had enjoyed today. She and Garth had done things together they hadn't done in years.

She could still hear music, which meant he hadn't gone to bed yet. Turning on her side, she opened the e-reader, while thinking about how he'd defined their relationship while they were here. They were not sharing space as employer and employee, but as friends.

Was there a reason he'd wanted to make that distinction?

She'd been serious when she brought up the issue of the woman who was to have met him here. Not all women, or men, would be so understanding. Regan couldn't claim that she would be. But she would let him handle his business.

Tomorrow they would have their space and maybe that was a good thing. Time would tell.

Garth stood and moved across the room to turn off the music. It was past midnight already. Shoving his hands into the pockets of his jeans, he threw his head back and inhaled deeply, drawing in Regan's lingering scent. She'd gone to bed hours ago, yet her scent was still here, and had stayed while the music played.

He had closed his eyes so his mind could absorb the music and his entire body could soak up her fragrance. He yearned for things he hadn't had in months and only wanted them with her.

That was the crux of his problem. He couldn't have them with her. This insane craving for her couldn't be normal, could it?

Why not? his mind countered. *She's beautiful and she's single. She told you she was not involved with that military guy any longer, so what's the problem? And tonight you defined your relationship as personal.*

He had enjoyed playing Scrabble with her and loved it whenever she had challenged him. Not because he'd known his word would stand, but because she was so intense about winning. It seemed his Regan had a few competitive genes, as well.

His Regan?

He frowned. She was not his, although tonight there had been a couple of times he'd thought of her as such.

Grabbing his wineglass, he stood and headed for the kitchen. Tomorrow they would do separate activities during the day. However, he had a feeling tomorrow night, attending the opera with her, would definitely be a test of his endurance.

Nine

Regan stood at the window and then looked down at her watch. It was almost six o'clock, and if she and Garth planned to attend the opera, they would need time to get dressed and leave at least by seven-thirty, since it began at eight.

"We're still going to the opera tonight, right?"

Regan jumped, startled. Turning, she saw Garth leaning against a pillar. She fought to keep her heart from racing. He was shirtless, with his jeans riding low on his hips. She'd seen him without a shirt before. Like yesterday, when they'd gone swimming, and at other times over the years. But that didn't mean a thing to her pulse rate.

"Where did you come from?" she asked him.

"My bedroom. I just woke up from my nap."

She could see that now. He still seemed drowsy around his eyes. The sleepy look was sexy on him. Way too sexy. "I didn't know you had returned from sailing."

"I came back three hours ago."

"Oh." That had to have been when she'd been in her bedroom talking on the phone to Simone...or rather listening to Simone, since her best friend had done all the talking.

Simone figured yesterday would have been a great day to seduce Garth. It had taken Regan a good half hour to reiterate to Simone she intended to do no such thing.

"So, are we still going to the opera?" he asked her.

"Yes, I still want to go."

"Then we will."

"Paulo left food for you if you're hungry."

"I'm not. I still feel full from those sandwiches he fixed me for lunch."

"How was sailing?"

"Great. I loved being out on the water. I had my music with me. It doesn't get any better than that."

She nodded. "Well, I'm glad you're getting rest, Garth."

He smiled. "You and Charm both. She called earlier and threatened to disown me if she finds out I'm working on files while I'm here."

Regan lifted a brow. She'd heard the music playing last night from her bedroom. Jazz. What he usually listened to while working. "Are you working on files from here, Garth?"

"Nope. This has been a relaxing trip so far. Besides, I wouldn't undermine Cash like that."

No, he wouldn't. "I'm sure Cash is doing just fine running things."

"I'm sure of that, too. If something comes up that needs my attention, he knows how to reach me." Garth glanced at his watch. "I guess it's time for us to get dressed. You want to meet back in this same spot in about an hour?"

"That sounds good," she said.

"The opera lasts three hours, followed by a reception with dancing."

"I saw that. Do you think you'll want to stay up that late?"

He chuckled. "Need I remind you that you're the one who goes to bed with the chickens. I should be the one asking you if you're okay with the late hour."

"I think dancing would be nice."

"So do I. Then let's do it," he said.

"Yes," she agreed. "Let's do it."

Regan looked radiant, Garth thought, watching her enter the room. She was so beautiful he was rendered speechless. He was grateful he had the pillar to lean on. Otherwise he would have gotten weak in the knees. With each graceful step she took, he was aware of her in every pore of his body. He could even feel blood rushing through his veins.

The gown she'd worn to the Westmoreland Charity Ball had knocked the breath out of his lungs. The one she had on tonight was having the same effect, tenfold. On top of that, the way it draped over her curves stirred sexual hunger to life in his midsection.

Even her hair was different. The curls were piled high, nearly forming a halo around her head. Regan was incredibly feminine from top to bottom, and the areas in between, he was certain. Her soft-as-sin curves were captivating his mind, making him appreciate being a man.

"I'm ready, Garth."

She might be ready, but he sure wasn't. Sharing space with her tonight would definitely be a distraction. A distraction he couldn't handle. "You look beautiful, Regan."

A smile spread across her face. "Just a little something I threw together."

If that was the case, and he figured it wasn't, she'd thrown it together rather nicely. "Well, no matter how you managed it, you look beautiful."

"Thanks, Garth."

Even her makeup looked good on her. She hadn't been heavy-handed with it. It was light and blended perfectly with her skin tone.

And speaking of skin…

Was that a split up the side of that gown? One that went up past her knee and over her thigh whenever she walked? One that flashed skin? A lot of skin? When she came to a stop in front of him, he stared down at her generous cleavage that revealed even more skin.

He inhaled deeply, then wished he hadn't. Her scent was even more of an attention-grabber tonight. It was getting to him in ways a female perfume never had before. Tonight, he'd been bitten.

"Ready for an enjoyable night?" he asked her, leading her to the door.

"Yes. I'm more than ready."

Three hours later, Garth glanced over at Regan, who was sitting beside him in the huge opera theater. The theater lights were turned down, which afforded him an opportunity to study her. It was obvious from the look on her face and the focus of her gaze that she was enjoying the opera.

And he was enjoying her.

He shifted to sit more comfortably in his seat. If he continued to stare at her, she would eventually notice. Though maybe not, since her attention was clearly on the singer who was performing on stage. Pretty soon it would be time for intermission. No sooner did that thought pop into his mind than the lights came on.

He used that time to walk around and stretch his legs while Regan visited the ladies' room. Moments later, they met back up and he suggested they stop by the concession area for coffee.

Garth tried not to notice the men admiring Regan in that beautiful gown she was wearing. The same gown that draped across her curves, her breasts, and clinched at the waist, showing a perfect hourglass figure. While he was in one line getting their coffee, she was in another grabbing snacks. He overheard the two men in line in front of him remark to each other about what a gorgeous woman she was and that they envied the lucky man she was with tonight.

They'd spoken not knowing Garth was fluent in Spanish and understood everything they said. He was tempted to tell them he was the lucky man. However, he figured they would find that out when they saw him and Regan together later.

He glanced over to where Regan sat after she'd gotten them a table. They had twenty minutes before the lights would start blinking, letting everyone know intermission was over and it was time to return to their seats.

He recalled the drive to the opera house. He'd ridden in a car with Regan numerous times, but tonight had felt different. She had kept the conversation lively by telling him she'd been asked to host a booth at a career fair at one of the schools next year. She made sure to mention that she'd only committed after checking his schedule to verify it was a day he wouldn't need her. Since she was thinking about his schedule that far in advance, he hoped that meant she wasn't giving Harold Anders's job offer any serious consideration.

He joined her at the table with two cups of coffee. "Here you are," he said, placing one in front of her.

"Thanks. Wasn't that singer superb?" she asked in an excited voice.

There was no way he would admit he hadn't paid attention to the singer since his mind had been filled with sexual thoughts of her. Sitting so close to her in the auditorium had played havoc on his libido. And when the lights had come on for intermission, he'd glanced down to see the split in her gown showing him a portion of her thigh. That hadn't helped matters.

"This coffee is good, Garth."

Her words intruded into his thoughts. Was it? He hadn't noticed even though he'd taken a couple of sips.

He'd been looking at how perfectly her lips fit on the cup as she tried not to smear her ruby-red lipstick.

There wasn't much about Regan that didn't turn him on, leaving him longing. He'd known it, yet he had still invited her to join him at the château for two weeks. How crazy was that when his prime purpose for coming here had been to put an end to his intense attraction to Regan by meeting up with another woman? Things hadn't turned out that way, and now his attraction had become red-hot desire.

He was faced with two choices. He could either handle it or act on it.

He wasn't sure how he would handle it, but his mind immediately filled with ways to act on it. There was no need to blame not having sex for so long as the reason for his horny thoughts. Deep down he knew that was just an excuse. He could have had any woman he'd wanted, and he needed to stop claiming he'd been way too busy for one. A man made time for what he wanted, and the truth of the matter was—he hadn't wanted another woman.

Not even the one chosen for him by the dating service. He had thought perhaps seeing her in person might create a spark. But now, he had a gut feeling it would not have. He'd sought the woman out for the wrong reasons. He was glad she hadn't shown up.

The lights began blinking.

"I guess that means it's time to go back. But first I want to thank you for bringing me tonight, Garth. For sharing all the activities with me for the last two days. I know I wasn't the one who was supposed to enjoy these things with you, and I might be wrong for feeling this way, but I'm glad I got to do them, even if I was a spare."

A spare? Was that how she saw it? How could she not? At that moment he decided to give her something else to think about. Meeting her gaze, he said, "There is no other woman I'd rather be here with than you, Regan."

There.

At that precise moment, he had made a decision.

He wouldn't handle his intense attraction to her. He intended to act on it.

There was no reason for him to continue fighting his desire. Regan was a grown woman who could make up her own mind about whether she would want an affair with him or not.

She smiled. "That's a kind thing to say, Garth."

He had a feeling she didn't believe him. That meant he had eleven days to convince her he'd meant every word.

Ten

There is no other woman I'd rather be here with than you, Regan...

Garth's words were still warming Regan's heart when the opera ended, and they entered the room where the reception would be held. Had he really meant what he said or was he just being kind?

"This place looks nice," Garth said, and in a surprise move, he took her hand in his and led her through the throng of people toward an empty table.

The moment their hands touched, sensations spread up her spine. She inwardly told herself the only reason her hand was in his larger one was because the room was crowded, and he wanted to make sure they stayed together. But what about the other times he'd held her hand tonight?

Once seated, she glanced around. The table was perfect. It was close to the dance floor and not far from a buffet of hors d'oeuvres. A live band performed an array of music that ranged from classical, jazz, Latin and even R&B. Several couples were already out on the dance floor.

"I'll go get our drinks. What would you like?" Garth asked her.

"A glass of red wine will be fine."

"Okay, I'll be back in a minute.

She watched him leave while thinking how nice he looked in his tux. Of course, she'd seen him in a tux before, but still… It showed off his broad shoulders, muscled chest, firm thighs and muscular arms. He was a specimen of a man that any woman would appreciate. She hadn't missed the number of women checking him out tonight.

She switched her attention from Garth and his admirers to the architectural beauty of the room. Beams and columns framed high chandeliers. The outside of the building was built in the form of a massive wave. It was beautiful and could rival the opera house in Sydney, Australia.

"If you're alone, senorita, I would love to join you," a deep male voice said.

Regan glanced up to see a tall, handsome man standing by her table. She was about to tell him that no, she wasn't alone, when a familiar, authoritative male voice answered. "She isn't alone. She's with me."

"I'm sorry, senor," the man said apologetically and quickly walked off.

Regan looked up at Garth and understood why the man had left so quickly. A fierce frown covered Garth's face. He handed her a wineglass before sliding into the chair beside her.

"Sorry I took so long," he said.

"You weren't gone long, and thanks for bringing me the wine," she said, wondering why he'd acted so protective of her just now. She recalled him doing the same thing at the Westmoreland Charity Ball several months ago. The last thing she wanted was for him to start treating her like he was her protector.

She took a sip of her wine. "I could have handled him, you know."

He met her gaze. "Yes, I know. However, when you're with me you don't have to."

She didn't say anything, deciding not to make an issue of it. "So, what's on the agenda for tomorrow?" she asked, to change the subject.

"Hiking."

She blinked. "Hiking?"

"Yes. Of course, you don't have to go. You can sleep in if you like. But if you decide to join me, it's best if we get an early start to beat the sun."

Regan stared at him. They probably wouldn't get home before midnight tonight, and he wanted to get up early? She didn't have a problem being an early riser, but usually she would be in the bed early the night before, as well.

"Do you want to dance?"

Since she knew they would be hiking tomorrow, it would have been a good idea to suggest they return to the château. However, a part of her refused to give up a chance to dance with him. "Yes."

Garth stood and offered her his hand. Placing her wineglass down, she took his hand and he led her to the dance floor. She felt a tingling sensation just from touching him. She knew things were about to get hotter being in his arms.

He drew her to him, and she felt comfortable with her body meshed to his. When he began moving, she automatically followed. She loved remembering the last time they'd danced together. Now, tonight, she would have new memories.

He still held her hand in his, against his chest. Seemingly against his heart. "Did you enjoy the opera?"

She looked up at him when she wanted more than anything to place her face on his chest and draw in his scent. "Yes, what about you?"

"Yes, but I admit to watching you a lot."

Her eyes widened. She hadn't known. "Why?"

"Seeing the happiness on your face was priceless. I could tell you were really enjoying yourself."

A smile spread across her lips. "Yes, I was. But it doesn't sound as if you were if you were watching me."

"I enjoy watching you."

She swallowed deeply. "Why?"

"I just do."

A part of her wanted to ask him to be more specific, but she decided not to. The music would be coming to an end soon and she wanted to savor being in his arms while dancing. He then placed his hands around her waist. Was she imagining things or were his fingers at her waist nudging their bodies closer? Or was her body just naturally moving closer to his?

The music was a slow Spanish concerto. Garth was an excellent dancer and she followed his lead. He'd said he enjoyed looking at her. Was there more to it than that? Was she wrong to hope there was? Was she wasting her time even thinking such a thing?

At that moment she really didn't want to spend a lot of time thinking. Instead she wanted to bask in the feel of being in his arms.

So she rested her head on his chest.

Garth glanced down at Regan. He liked the feel of her head resting against his shoulder. He doubted she knew how many times tonight he'd thought about kissing her. He had admitted to not being able to keep his eyes off her and that would have been the perfect opportunity for him to tell her how much he desired her, ached for her.

But he hadn't.

However, he would—just not now, not here.

He was tired of resisting.

She lifted her head from his chest and her gaze locked with his. For the longest time, they stared at each other. Sexual hunger took over every part of his being. Surrendering to a primitive force he could no longer fight, he lowered his head to hers. Their mouths were a breath apart when he felt a tap on his shoulder. He swung his head around.

"May I cut in?"

Maybe Garth should have felt grateful that the man's

untimely arrival had stopped him from kissing Regan in the middle of the dance floor, but he didn't. All he felt was a high degree of annoyance. "No, you can't."

Dismissing the man's presence, Garth turned to Regan. "I'm ready to leave."

She nodded. "So am I."

Twenty minutes later, Garth brought the car to a stop in front of the château. He noticed Regan hadn't said anything since leaving the opera house. Was she upset with him for behaving like a Neanderthal with that guy who'd wanted to dance with her? Acting territorial, as if he had every right to do so?

"Are you upset with me?" he asked. He wanted to know now, before they went inside.

She glanced over at him. "No, although I don't understand why you feel the need to act like my protector."

Was that what she thought? Even when he'd come within a moment of kissing her? "I wasn't acting like your protector, Regan."

"Then what?"

He broke eye contact to draw in a deep breath. She had to know, or at least suspect, he desired her. Was she waiting for him to spell things out? If so, then he would. "We'll talk about it when we get inside. Okay?"

She nodded. "Okay."

He got out of the car to open the passenger door for her. Then he took her hand in his, and they walked to the front entrance. He let them inside.

"I'd love a cup of coffee while we talk. What about you?" he asked her.

"Yes, I'd love a cup, too, but first I'd like to get out of this gown and shoes. Could you give me ten minutes?"

He nodded as a vision of her getting out of the gown and shoes filtered through his mind. "Yes, I could use ten minutes, as well."

Garth noted he was still holding her hand. Looking down at their joined hands, he lifted them to his lips. That wasn't enough. Releasing their hands, he placed his at her waist while staring down at her. He needed to do the one thing he'd almost done on that dance floor. The one thing he'd dreamed of doing to those lips for quite some time.

"Garth?"

He saw mixed emotions in her gaze and knew there was only one remedy. He lowered his head to hers.

She released a moan the moment their mouths connected. He heard it and the sound shook him to the core. When their tongues mingled, dueling like they couldn't get enough of each other, his control shattered.

Tightening his arms around her waist, he drew her closer as he deepened the kiss in a way that had him moaning right along with her. He was deliberately mating their mouths and he didn't want her to concentrate on anything other than the way his tongue was stroking hers. Fire stirred in his loins, arousing him in ways he hadn't experienced in years, if ever.

Knowing they couldn't stand here and kiss forever—although he wished like hell they could—he reluctantly brought the kiss to an end. He saw the desire in her gaze and was tempted to kiss her again. Instead he said, "We meet back here in ten minutes, right?" He dropped his hands from her waist and slowly backed up.

"Can we make it twenty?" she said softly, as she also began slowly backing away.

"Yes."

She turned and quickly walked to her bedroom and he walked toward his. Entering the bedroom, he eased the tuxedo jacket from his shoulders and then removed his tie. He wondered if Regan still thought he was acting like a protector. Would a protector kiss her the way he just had? He couldn't help wondering what she was thinking right about now.

Regan leaned against the bedroom door. Breathing in deeply to slow down the wild beating of her heart, struggling to come to terms with what had just happened.

Garth had kissed her. He had actually kissed her.

Nobody knew the number of times she had fantasized about him doing what he'd just done. Should she pinch herself to make sure she wasn't dreaming? Should she regret it, since technically he was her boss? Common sense told her that maybe she should do both of those things, but common sense was something she lacked right now.

She moved away from the door to the mirror on the wall to take a look at her reflection. Namely, her mouth. She smiled when she saw a pair of lips that had been thoroughly kissed by Garth Bartram Outlaw. A kiss that had shaken every nerve in her body. Even now, she felt her insides quivering.

Moving from the mirror, she slid out of her shoes

and then danced around the room, on top of the world. What had Garth meant by the kiss? He had certainly put to rest her assumption that he'd been acting like her protector. As far as she was concerned, Garth was the epitome of every woman's fantasy. He'd certainly been hers. No matter how many guys she'd dated, they hadn't been Garth. No guy had held a light to him. None.

But what had that kiss meant? Was it just his testosterone acting up or could it mean more?

As she slid out of her gown, she hoped it was more. She traced her lips with her tongue. Yes, definitely she wanted more. But, she had to be realistic. She had to think about what *more* would entail. Yet, at the moment, she didn't want to think at all.

She glanced at her watch. She now had less than ten minutes to redress. What would they talk about? Would he tell her he'd decided after all this time that he loved her and—

Regan suddenly went still. She needed to calm down and stop acting like a sixteen-year-old who'd gotten kissed by the most popular boy in school. She had to stop thinking about things that might not happen…like another kiss, the feel of his hands all over her, him stripping off her clothes, taking her against that pillar he liked leaning against.

She needed to pull herself together, and no matter how difficult that might be, she would do it.

Precisely twenty minutes later, after changing into a pair of jeans and a shirt, Garth returned to the foyer just as Regan did. He nearly missed a step when he saw the outfit she'd changed into. It was a beautiful jumpsuit with an off-the-shoulder neckline that emphasized the curve of her neck.

His gaze traveled up to her face and zeroed in on her mouth, the lips he'd tasted earlier. She had applied more lipstick. He fought the urge to close the distance between them and kiss it off.

While getting undressed, several alarming thoughts had filled his mind. What if Regan wasn't ready for what he wanted? If he were to let his desires be known and they weren't reciprocated, it could push her toward ending her employment with the company. If he proposed an affair, things could get messy if it didn't work out. It would not only ruin his relationship with her, but also with Franklin. Could he risk all of that?

"There are a couple of Paulo's muffins left from this morning. I plan to grab one. Would you want one, as well?" she asked as they walked side by side to the kitchen. "I bet it would go well with the coffee."

He picked up on the slight nervousness in her voice. He didn't want her to feel uneasy around him. He would do and say whatever it took to remove any tension between them.

"I bet so, too, but I'll pass. I had enough sweets for the night. Go ahead and grab your muffin and I'll get the coffee started," he said in a lighthearted tone.

"Okay."

He moved to the counter where the coffeepot sat and couldn't resist glancing over at her as she moved toward the refrigerator. That outfit looked pretty damn nice on her. In fact, she looked good in anything she put on her body…even her pilot uniform. But what was on his mind now, more than anything, was her taste. No woman's mouth had a right to taste as delectable as hers had tasted.

Garth returned his attention to the coffeepot, wondering what he would say when they sat down to talk. He heard the movement behind him and fought the urge to look over his shoulder again. Was she thinking about the kiss as much as he was? Had she enjoyed it as much? Did she want to do it again? When the aroma of cinnamon floated across the kitchen to where he stood, he figured she was warming her muffin up in the microwave. A part of him wished she would come over and warm him up, too. In his present state, it wouldn't take much.

By the time he poured the coffee into cups and headed for the table, she was sitting there waiting. He forced a smile onto his features. Now he was the one feeling nervous. "I guess going hiking with me in the morning is off the table. It's after midnight," he said, placing the coffee cup in front of her, and then sitting down with his own.

She shrugged her shoulders—those beautiful shoulders left bare in the outfit she was wearing. "Who knows? I might surprise you." Then, taking a sip of her coffee, she said, "Mmm, you have the magic touch when it comes to making coffee, Garth."

He chuckled. She'd always told him that, which was why she left the making of the coffee on the plane to him. He would make a pot before the jet took off, and by the time it leveled off in the sky, he was ready for a cup. He would also take a cup to her in the cockpit.

He watched her take a bite out of the muffin. She looked over at him, catching him staring. She licked a few crumbs from around her lips. "You sure you don't want me to warm one up for you? It's delicious."

"Yes, I'd like one, but just a taste. May I have a bite of yours?"

He wasn't sure whether or not his question surprised her. Her expression was unreadable. She lifted the muffin to his mouth and he took his own bite, in the very spot where she'd taken hers. Then he licked the crumbs off his lips, knowing she was watching him.

"You might be right after all, Regan," he said. His gaze held hers, and he could see the pulse in her throat beating rapidly.

"Right about what?"

"Kidnapping Paulo."

A smile spread across her lips. "Think we can come up with a plan?" she asked, finishing off the muffin.

Watching her, knowing they'd shared that muffin, made intense desire heat his core. "With us together, Regan, anything is possible."

His words must have stirred something within her because he saw the pulse racing in her throat again. She took a sip of her coffee and then sat the cup down and looked at him. She licked her lips, which caused a hard jolt of need to pass through him. He picked up his cup to take a sip of his own coffee, wishing it was something stronger.

"You said we would talk, Garth."

Placing his cup down, he met her gaze. "What I have to say can be summed up in a few words, Regan."

She raised a brow. "And what words are those?"

"I want you."

One Minute" Survey

You get up to **FOUR books**
<u>and</u> TWO Mystery Gifts...

ABSOLUTELY FREE!

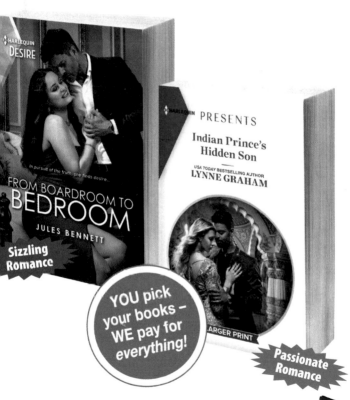

HARLEQUIN DESIRE

In pursuit of the truth, she finds desire...

FROM BOARDROOM TO BEDROOM

JULES BENNETT

Sizzling Romance

HARLEQUIN PRESENTS

Indian Prince's Hidden Son

USA TODAY BESTSELLING AUTHOR
LYNNE GRAHAM

LARGER PRINT

Passionate Romance

YOU pick your books – WE pay for everything!

See inside for details.

YOU pick your books –
WE pay for everything.
You get up to FOUR new books and TWO Mystery Gift
absolutely FREE!
Total retail value: Over $20!

Dear Reader,

Your opinions are important to us. So if you'll participate in our fa
and free "One Minute" Survey, **YOU** can pick up to four wonderf
books that **WE** pay for!

As a leading publisher of women's fiction, we'd love to hear from
you. That's why we promise to reward you for completing our
survey.

IMPORTANT: Please complete the survey and return it. We'll sen
your Free Books and Free Mystery Gifts right away. **And we pay
for shipping and handling too!** ← *We pay for EVERYTHING!*

Try **Harlequin® Desire** books featuring the worlds of the
American elite with juicy plot twists, delicious sensuality and
intriguing scandal.

Try **Harlequin Presents® Larger-Print** books featuring the
glamourous lives of royals and billionaires in a world of exotic
locations, where passion knows no bounds.

Or TRY BOTH!

Thank you again for participating in our "One Minute"
Survey. It really takes just a minute (or less) to complete the
survey… and your free books and gifts will be well worth it!

Sincerely,

Pam Powers

Pam Powers
for Reader Service

www.ReaderService.co

"One Minute" Survey

GET YOUR FREE BOOKS AND FREE GIFTS!

✓ Complete this Survey   ✓ Return this survey

◄ DETACH AND MAIL CARD TODAY! ▼

1 Do you try to find time to read every day?

☐ YES   ☐ NO

2 Do you prefer stories with happy endings?

☐ YES   ☐ NO

3 Do you enjoy having books delivered to your home?

☐ YES   ☐ NO

4 Do you find a Larger Print size easier on your eyes?

☐ YES   ☐ NO

YES! I have completed the above "One Minute" Survey. Please send me my Free Books and Free Mystery Gifts (worth over $20 retail). I understand that I am under no obligation to buy anything, as explained on the back of this card.

☐ I prefer Harlequin® Desire 225/326 HDL GNWS

☐ I prefer Harlequin Presents® Larger Print 176 /376 HDL GNWS

☐ I prefer BOTH 225/326 & 176/376 HDL GNW4

FIRST NAME

LAST NAME

ADDRESS

APT.#

CITY

STATE/PROV.

ZIP/POSTAL CODE

© 2019 HARLEQUIN ENTERPRISES ULC
™ and ® are trademarks owned by Harlequin Enterprises ULC. Printed in the U.S.A.

Offer limited to one per household and not applicable to series that subscriber is currently receiving.
Your Privacy—The Reader Service is committed to protecting your privacy. Our Privacy Policy is available online at www.ReaderService.com or upon request from the Reader Service. We make a portion of our mailing list available to reputable third parties that offer products we believe may interest you. If you prefer that we not exchange your name with third parties, or if you wish to clarify or modify your communication preferences, please visit us at www.ReaderService.com/consumerschoice or write to us at Reader Service Preference Service, P.O. Box 9062, Buffalo, NY 14240-9062. Include your complete name and address.   HD/HP-520-OM20

READER SERVICE—Here's how it works:

Accepting your 2 free books and 2 free gifts (gifts valued at approximately $10.00 retail) places you under no obligation to buy anything. You may keep the books and gifts and return the shipping statement marked "cancel." If you do not cancel, approximately one month later we'll send you more books from the series you have chosen, and bill you at our low, subscribers-only discount price. Harlequin Presents® Larger-Print books consist of 6 books each month and cost $5.80 each in the U.S. or $5.99 each in Canada, a savings of at least 11% off the cover price. Harlequin Desire® books consist of 6 books each month and cost just $4.55 each in the U.S. or $5.24 each in Canada, a savings of at least 13% off the cover price. It's quite a bargain! Shipping and handling is just 50¢ per book in the U.S. and $1.25 per book in Canada*. You may return any shipment at our expense and cancel at any time — or you may continue to receive monthly shipments at our low, subscribers-only discount price plus shipping and handling. *Terms and prices subject to change without notice. Prices do not include sales taxes which will be charged (if applicable) based on your state or country of residence. Canadian residents will be charged applicable taxes. Offer not valid in Quebec. Books received may not be as shown. All orders subject to approval. Credit or debit balances in a customer's account(s) may be offset by any other outstanding balance owed by or to the customer. Please allow 3 to 4 weeks for delivery. Offer available while quantities last.

▼ If offer card is missing write to: Reader Service, P.O. Box 1341, Buffalo, NY 14240-8531 or visit www.ReaderService.com ▼

BUSINESS REPLY MAIL
FIRST-CLASS MAIL   PERMIT NO. 717   BUFFALO, NY

POSTAGE WILL BE PAID BY ADDRESSEE

READER SERVICE
PO BOX 1341
BUFFALO NY 14240-8571

NO POSTAGE
NECESSARY
IF MAILED
IN THE
UNITED STATES

Eleven

Sensuous shivers spread through Regan as she stared at Garth, speechless. First off, the kiss; then he'd shared that muffin with her. And now…

Granted, she'd known he was a straight shooter. However, she hadn't expected what he'd just said.

He wanted her?

"Yes, I want you," he said again, when she didn't respond. "I figured that kiss would have been a good indicator."

She drew in a deep breath. It had been, but still… "I worked for you for almost five years, and you never paid me any attention, Garth."

He leaned back in his chair as he picked up his coffee cup again to take a sip. "If you recall, Regan, after losing Karen, I wasn't paying any woman much attention. I barely dated."

As far as she was concerned, he barely dated now, and when he did, she figured it was to take care of his physical needs. "So why now and why me?"

"Why not you, Regan? You are a very beautiful woman."

She rolled her eyes. "I look the same as I've always looked, Garth."

"That might be the case, but I began truly noticing your looks a few months ago. I guess you can say my blinders were taken off."

She took a sip of her coffee and met his gaze over the cup. "And just when were these blinders removed?"

"The night of the Westmoreland Charity Ball."

She placed her cup down, remembering that night. He had surprised her by inviting her to go with him. She'd discovered later that Bailey, whom Regan had gotten to know after Bailey married Walker, had suggested that he bring Regan. She also recalled he'd been very attentive that night. Even his brothers had teased him about it.

"Do you remember that night?" he asked her.

She nodded. "Yes, I remember. I thought you were being overprotective."

"You assumed that tonight, as well. You were wrong both times, Regan. Both times I was being territorial. That night I felt something that I hadn't felt in ten years. Sexual attraction toward a woman, of a magnitude that it was hard for me think straight. It made me want to take you somewhere and seduce you."

She blinked, finding what he was saying hard to be-lieve. "Seriously?"

A smile curved his lips. "Yes, seriously."

Regan took another sip of her coffee. Then with a boldness that surprised even her, she asked, "Why didn't you seduce me, Garth?"

She saw the flash of heat that appeared in his eyes. He quickly took another sip of his coffee. "There's no way I could have done that," he finally said.

She lifted a brow. "Why not?"

"The man who seduces you should be the man who plans to marry you. You would expect that."

He was right. Gone were the days when she was into sex for the sake of sex. She was older, wiser and a lot more mature than she'd been in her early twenties. At twenty-eight, she wanted more from a relationship. For her, being intimate with a man meant marriage was in their future. That was one of the reasons she hadn't slept with Craig. In addition to him being the suspicious and jealous type, she hadn't loved him.

Was Garth letting her know any seduction on his part would be nothing more than casual sex? If that was true, had he planned to spend two weeks with a woman he wasn't serious about? Would his affair with that other woman have been nothing more than sex?

"Are you saying you're not interested in getting mar-ried ever, Garth?"

He shook his head. "No, that's not what I'm saying. In fact, I've been thinking about marriage a lot lately."

Hope sprang up inside of Regan. "You have?"

"Yes. In fact, that's the reason I came to Santa Cruz.

I was to meet a woman I was contemplating marrying one day."

Regan's hope was replaced by disappointment and confusion. "Let me get this straight. The woman you were to meet here, the one who eventually was a no-show—you were thinking about marrying her?"

"Yes."

"But now you want me?"

"Yes."

She frowned. That didn't make sense. For him to think about marrying a woman meant that he and the woman were in love and sharing a serious relationship. If that was the case, then how could he tell Regan that he wanted *her*? Did he not think that was betraying the woman he planned to marry? Did he assume Regan would just step right in and take the woman's place in his bed? She expected better of him.

"Sorry to disappoint you, Garth," she said in a curt tone, standing to her feet. "There are some substitutions I will not do."

He reached out and took her hand. When she tried pulling it back, he tightened his grip. "I think you might have misunderstood me, Regan. Please sit back down so I can explain."

Regan wasn't sure what he could explain, but the feel of his hand touching hers caused all kinds of sensations to curl around in her stomach. She sat back down. Not because he'd requested it, but because she felt weak in the knees from his touch.

She lifted her chin. "You kissed me and said you wanted me. Yet, now you're telling me the woman you were to spend two weeks with here was someone you might marry. So, what did I misunderstand, Garth?"

Garth had made a mess of things, when all he'd been trying to do was have a totally honest discussion with Regan. But her assumption was pretty damn damaging. There was a lot she needed to understand.

"First of all, I don't expect you to take anybody's place in my bed, Regan. To be honest, the woman who was supposed to meet me here would have been taking *your* place. It was *you* who I originally wanted in my bed."

"What? You definitely need to explain that, Garth."

A part of Garth wished he hadn't been so blunt. But he had, and now he owed her an explanation. "My reaction to you that night in Denver, at the ball, bothered me. Like I said, it was the first time in nearly ten years I had felt such strong attraction to a woman. It also made me realize something else."

"What?"

"That you weren't Franklin's little girl anymore or Charm's teenage bestie. You had grown up to become a very beautiful woman."

She shrugged. "Not sure about the beautiful part, Garth, but I've been a woman for quite a while now."

"I honestly hadn't noticed you that way. But that night…your dress, the hair, the makeup, the total package…" He paused a moment. "Especially that dress. You were wearing the hell out of it."

"Thanks. I'll take that as a compliment, but it still doesn't explain things."

He nodded. "After we returned to Alaska we picked

up our normal routine. I figured my attraction to you that night was one and done. But that wasn't the case. My desire for you grew stronger, taking over my mind and senses, interfering with the way I handled business matters. I knew I had to do something. That's when I came up with a plan."

"And what was this plan?"

"To turn my attention elsewhere. That meant meeting someone I could get serious about since I considered you off-limits."

She took a sip of her coffee before asking, "So how did you meet this 'someone else'?"

He shifted in his seat, deciding he might as well tell her everything. "Through a very private dating service. And for the record, we never officially met. Santa Cruz was to be our first meeting."

Garth and the woman hadn't met?

Regan was surprised. She had used an online dating service before, so she knew how it worked.

"So, if the two of you would have clicked, then you would have considered her wife material?" she asked, trying to understand. The Garth Outlaw she knew preferred handling his own personal affairs, and she would think that would include selecting the woman he might end up sharing his life with.

"Yes, and before you make more assumptions, I was pretty detailed in my specifications. They are thorough when vetting people and have an exclusive clientele. Their match for me rated highly and I thought she might be perfect."

Regan was trying hard to keep her composure when her heart was breaking. "Yet your perfect woman didn't show."

"No, but it wasn't her fault. It was a dating service error. Somehow there was a mix-up on dates."

"But you will reschedule?"

He shook his head. "No, I won't. Her not showing up was a good thing."

Regan glanced over at him. "Why?"

"Because I was only using her to help me get over my attraction to you. I see now that would not have been fair. And over these last few days, my desire for you has only increased. In fact, I can truthfully say that I desire you more than I've ever desired any woman before."

She fought back the hope that tried to return. She wondered if he realized the power of what he'd just said. What she still didn't understand, though, was why he'd felt he couldn't act on his attraction to Regan. Why had he gone to all the trouble of finding someone else?

"You were contemplating marrying her had the two of you hit it off?" she asked again.

"Yes. And there is one thing you need to know, Regan."

"What?" she asked past the lump suddenly forming in her throat.

He leaned forward in his chair and held her gaze. It was as if what he was about to say was highly important. She had a feeling that, whatever it was, she was not going to like it.

"What is it, Garth?"

"Whereas I was willing to marry another woman, I am not willing to marry you."

Twelve

Regan snatched her hand from his as if she'd been physically slapped. She felt like she had been. Did he think she was not good enough for him?

As if he read her thoughts again, he said, "Let me explain—"

"You did already," she said, pushing her chair away from the table. "I got it. I'm good enough to sleep with but not good enough to marry. Can't have you marrying the hired help, right?"

"Damn it, Regan, that's not it and you know it. How can you say something like that?"

He honestly had the nerve to ask her that after what he'd said? "I say it because you're insinuating it."

"No, I'm not. I would marry you if I could, but I can't."

That didn't make sense. "And why not?"

He paused for a long moment. "My ability to love any woman ended the day Karen died. The woman I was to meet here knew that and was willing to accept a loveless marriage, but I don't expect you to accept one. I wouldn't want you to. You deserve better. You deserve to marry a man who will love you the way you should be loved. I wish I could be that man, but I can't. My heart will always belong to Karen."

He sighed deeply. "I'm being totally honest with you, Regan. I want you, but I can't love you, or any woman. All I have to offer is an affair that you won't forget or regret."

"For me that's not good enough, Garth." She then left the kitchen and headed toward her bedroom.

Regan forced herself to keep walking and not look back. She should be angry with him, but she was only angry with herself for loving him so much and believing that one day he would notice her existence and love her back.

But he couldn't love her.

She had heard something similar before…from her father. How many times had Franklin Fairchild told her that he still loved her mother and that no other woman would have his heart?

Regan would tell Garth the same thing she'd told her father more than once. He was a man with a lot of love to give and she knew the woman he'd lost would want him to move on with his life and love again.

Those words had fallen on deaf ears with her father, and she knew they would with Garth, as well.

Entering her bedroom, she closed the door behind her, tempted to throw herself against it and cry until she couldn't cry anymore. But she refused to do that, because something Garth said tonight stuck out in her mind…

"I desire you more than I've ever desired any woman before."

Did he truly mean that? And if he did mean it, did it mean he desired her more than he had Karen? She began pacing. When he and Karen had met and fallen in love, Garth had been about the same age Regan was now. From what Charm had told her, it was a whirlwind romance when the two had been stationed in Syria. Regan figured he had to have fallen deeply in love for him to still feel that way ten years later.

He'd said that if and when he did marry, it would not be for love. Some women would settle for that. Hell, a lot of them did.

Could Regan do the same?

She stopped pacing and sat on the edge of her bed. What about couples who didn't marry for love, but then the love came later? She knew of one such couple. Agatha Meadows was one of Regan's college friends. Agatha and Christopher had met on a cruise and were intensely attracted to each other. They'd engaged in a hot and heavy affair onboard the ship, and after the cruise, they'd gone their separate ways—without so much as an exchange of phone numbers to keep in touch.

Two months later, Agatha had discovered she was pregnant. Believing Christopher had a right to know he'd fathered a child, she'd hired a private investigator to find him so she could give him the news. Christopher, elated at the thought of being a father, had convinced Agatha to enter into a loveless marriage for the sake of their unborn child. That had been a hard decision for Agatha to make since she'd dreamed of marrying one day for love.

She'd told Regan she would settle on desire rather than love because there was no doubt in her mind that she and Chris desired each other. In fact, Agatha was convinced their desire for each other had been the catalyst to them falling in love. Now, after nearly seven years of marriage and two children, Agatha would be the first to tell you that their desire for each other had transformed into love. They'd been determined to make the marriage work and it had blossomed into something neither had expected.

Granted, the situation with Garth was different from expecting a child together, but one aspect of their situation was similar. By his own admission he wanted her, and he had been willing to use another woman to get over his attraction to Regan. He'd even admitted that since being here with her, his desire for her had only increased. A part of her felt good knowing that, for the time being, she and she alone was the woman Garth wanted. The thought of that shouldn't make her heart swell, but it did. It gave her hope. Hope that what could start off as purely sexual could blossom into something more.

Regan began pacing again. Would any other woman fight for something more with Garth? Just like Garth thought Regan should marry for love, she thought he should marry for love, as well—even if that love was one-sided.

That was what he didn't know. She loved him.

Now she needed to somehow convince him that the woman he wanted could also become the wife he needed. The wife who could show him how to love again. He didn't need to marry someone from some dating agency, or any other woman for that matter. He needed to marry *her*. She knew him. Understood him. And more important, she loved him.

It was time she fought for the man she loved.

Now she needed to come up with a strategy to make things work in her favor. For the past five years she'd worked for Garth as his private pilot. Those times she doubled as his private chauffeur, she'd had a listening ear to how he transacted business while in the back seat of a limo. He was a brilliant strategist, so she'd learned from the best. Now she could put that knowledge into action.

She would use his desire to her advantage. She'd build on his desire and go from there. Regan was about to embark on one of the most important missions of her life. She had never seduced a man before, but she'd read enough romance novels to have an idea about how it was done.

What if she failed? What if he never loved her? Knowing Garth, he would still do all the things that would truly matter, for the woman he chose as his wife. He would respect her, be faithful to her, honor her and protect her. In his own way, he would even adore her, although he might not ever truly love her.

Regan decided then and there that even if Garth never fell in love with her, she had enough love for the both of them.

Garth paced his bedroom knowing he'd blown things with Regan. It wouldn't surprise him if she was in her bedroom packing. How could he have been so stupid to admit something like that to her in the name of being honest.

No matter how he'd tried explaining things to her, it had gone from bad to worse. He wouldn't be surprised if she took Harold Anders's job offer now. Hell, it would serve Garth right if she did.

He stopped pacing. He needed to talk to someone, confess to being stupid and have that person agree with him. Pulling his phone out of his back pocket, he called Walker.

"Hello?"

"You awake, Walker?"

"Awake? Man, it's daytime here."

Garth had forgotten about the time difference. "I forgot."

"Whatever. And since I know it's nighttime there, is there a reason you're calling me and not in bed with that woman? The one you met through the dating service?"

"She didn't show due to a mix-up in dates."

"Oh. So now you're alone and bored with nothing to do."

"I'm not exactly alone. Regan's here with me."

"Regan is always with you, Garth. She's your pilot." Walker didn't get his meaning. "Regan was to leave after dropping me off and then come back for me in two weeks. I convinced her to stay."

"Oh."

He still wasn't sure Walker got it. "I want her, Walker. I want Regan."

His best friend laughed. Walker was honestly laughing.

"What the hell is so funny?" Garth asked.

"You. It took you long enough to figure that out, Garth. You don't think I haven't noticed that you want Regan? Hell, even Bailey noticed it. Why do you think she suggested you invite Regan to the Westmoreland Charity Ball?"

Garth rolled his eyes. "That's not possible. I only started wanting Regan at that ball."

"Wrong."

Garth frowned. "Wrong?"

"Yes, wrong. I began noticing how taken you were with Regan long before then. It might have been the night of that charity ball before you finally admitted it to yourself, but trust me. It's been long before that night. A year or so before. Maybe even longer."

Garth's frown deepened. Had it? As if Walker could read his mind, he said, "Trust me, Garth. I'm your best friend. I notice things, especially when they concern you."

"Then why the hell didn't you say something?"

Walker chuckled. "It wasn't my place. Besides, I was dealing with my own issues with Bailey. If you recall, I was fighting my own battles against falling in love. I didn't have the time or inclination to take on yours."

Garth leaned against the dresser in his room. "Love? Who said anything about love? I want Regan. I didn't say anything about loving her. You of all people know I could never love any woman but Karen."

Walker didn't say anything for a minute. "So, why are you calling?"

Garth rubbed his hands down his face. "I told you. I want Regan. Desire got the best of me. With us under the same roof, I told her I wanted her."

"And?"

"And I also told her all I wanted was an affair and nothing more."

"Okay. That's fair. You told her what to expect and what not to expect, which is what all men should do with women. So, what's the problem? Regan is a grown woman. She either agrees to the affair or she doesn't."

"That's not all I told her."

"What else did you say?"

"I told her that the woman who didn't show up here, the one from the dating service, was someone I had contemplated marrying."

"And?"

"And that although I wanted Regan way more than I wanted that woman, I could not consider marrying her."

"You actually told Regan that?"

"Yes, but I tried to explain why. I don't want Regan to settle for a loveless marriage. She deserves more."

"I agree Regan deserves more, but I think you made a mistake in telling her that. Think about it, Garth. You're willing to marry a woman you're not even sure you'd want. Yet you know you want Regan, but aren't willing to marry her."

"I told you why."

"Yes, and if you'll recall, after Kalyn, I swore I would never fall in love again, either."

"Our situations are different, Walker."

"I've discovered a person's heart can expand to include others if they're willing to let them in."

Garth threw his head back and closed his eyes. Those would be emotions he never wanted to feel again. Emotions he doubted he *could* feel. "I can't."

"You can't, Garth? Or you won't? Think about it."

Thirteen

"Good morning, Garth."

The hot coffee nearly scalded Garth's tongue. Regan had entered the kitchen wearing a pair of skintight leggings and a long pullover top. Her hair was pinned up on her head with a few ringlets around her face. Why did she have to look so desirable this morning? So darn refreshed? On top of that, she smelled so darn good. She looked nothing like he felt, which was absolutely lousy.

After talking to Walker, he hadn't gotten much sleep. He felt even more like an ass for asking her to sleep with him when there would be no benefit for her other than the promise of great sex. Regardless of what Walker had insinuated, only one woman could or would ever have his heart.

"Good morning, Regan. I hope you slept well," he said, studying her and trying to decipher her mood.

"I slept great. I see Paulo's been here," she replied, checking out the platters of food Paulo had left warming on the stove.

He was about to answer when she moved to lift a lid and a shaft of sunlight came through the window blinds. The ray of light seemed to shine directly on her. She looked even more beautiful then. He couldn't help noticing the shape of her face from this angle, how refined it looked and what a graceful pair of shoulders she had. He had noticed those same shoulders last night and had wanted to place kisses all over them. He still did.

She'd obviously expected him to say something. But when he didn't, she glanced over at him and caught him staring, and he couldn't pretend he hadn't been.

Lifting a brow, she asked, "Is something wrong, Garth?"

He swallowed deeply. So much for trying to maintain his control with her today. "No, nothing is wrong." Then trying to regain his common sense, he added, "You might want to try the baked cinnamon apples. They're good."

"Um, I think I will."

He broke eye contact to resume eating, but he was aware of every move she made around the kitchen. She finally came to the table and sat down, taking the same chair she'd sat in last night.

"I guess you didn't go hiking after all," she said, after saying grace.

"No. I decided to put it off for another day." He was

trying like hell to decipher her mood. He was convinced that when she'd left him in the kitchen last night, she'd been madder than hell. Now it was as if their conversation had never taken place. As if he hadn't proposed having an affair with her. Was she going to pretend it had never happened?

"About last night, Garth…"

Maybe she wasn't.

"Yes, what about it?"

"Your proposition. What time frame are you talking about for the affair, Garth?"

Did that mean she was considering it? A certain part of his anatomy wanted to leap for joy, but he refused to let it. "That will be up to you, Regan. Whatever you decide. However, if you decide to extend it beyond our time here, there's something you'll need to consider."

"What?"

"Are you willing for the affair to go public? You work for me and the last thing I want to do is to tarnish your good name. I couldn't do that to you."

"So, you would want us to sneak around?"

He could tell by her accusing tone that was honestly what she thought. "No. It wouldn't bother me if anyone knew we were seeing each other. I was merely thinking of your reputation, Regan. I don't want to hurt you in any way. I feel like a selfish ass even suggesting we have an affair, but…"

"But what, Garth?"

"I desire you more than I've ever desired any woman before. I should be able to walk away, but I can't. And that kiss we shared last night only made things worse."

"You said that last night and that's what I don't understand. You claim you desire me more than any woman before. Does that include Karen?"

He didn't say anything for a long while. She had every right to ask that. Hopefully, he would be able to explain and do a better job than he had last night. "Karen and I connected on a level beyond sexual chemistry. The desire was there, but not of this magnitude. When you're somewhere defending your country, desire and passion have to be placed on the back burner."

He paused. "There's nothing sexy about combat uniforms and fatigues. Karen and I managed a few stolen moments, but not many. We knew our situation was only temporary and there would be more time for the physical once our deployment ended and we returned to the States. That never happened, but there is no doubt in my mind that had Karen lived, and we had married, my desire for her would be a hell of a lot greater than what I feel for you, because she would have been my wife."

She didn't say anything, just continued to look at him. He couldn't help but wonder if his explanation had made things even worse.

"Thanks for explaining that, Garth. I fully understand now and I've made a decision."

He swallowed. "And what have you decided?"

"I will have an affair with you, Garth. However, it has to be short-term, only while we are here. Like you said, I have a reputation to protect."

He nodded. "Can I ask how you reached your decision?"

"Yes. You want me, and I want you, as well. More

than I've ever wanted any man. I know what we're feeling is just a physical thing based on sexual need. Therefore, I need to get it on with you and move on."

Get it on with him and move on?

Move on to where? To whom? Did it matter as long as he spent time with her? If she could handle the type of relationship he'd proposed, shouldn't that be all that mattered?

"Are you sure about this, Regan?"

A smile touched her lips. "I'm sure. But I do need the name of that dating service you used."

He nearly choked on his coffee. "Why?"

"I'm thinking of giving them a try," she said, biting into one of the baked apples.

"Clearly, you're joking."

"Why would I be joking?"

"Because I told you about the women who apply to that agency."

She nodded. "Yes, women looking for a future with a man who would suit them and vice versa. I found the whole thing fascinating. I did online dating a few years ago and it was a total disaster. The guy wasn't at all what I thought he would be."

"Then why try it again?"

"Because according to you, this dating service is good at vetting people and they have an exclusive clientele. That's what I want. It sounds like their male clients would be of the caliber I'd like to meet."

He scoffed at that. "You need to meet someone who will fall in love with you, Regan."

"Is there a reason you think I won't? Do you think a man can't fall in love with me?"

"That's not what I'm saying," he said, trying not to grit his teeth.

"Then what are you saying, Garth?"

That was a good question. "Nothing."

She frowned at him. "No, I think you *were* trying to say something."

Garth broke eye contact with Regan. The last thing he wanted was to make her mad with him. He knew she dated, so why would it bother him how she went about obtaining those dates? She had every right to use that dating service if that was what she wanted to do.

"You know what I think, Garth?"

He looked back over at her. She was still frowning. "No, Regan, what do you think?"

"I think you assume I'm not good enough to go through that agency. That the women who do are polished, refined and sophisticated and you can't see me as any of those things. You can't see me as a wife to any of those men."

"That's not true."

"I think it is. Need I remind you that I went to an all-girls private school until I was sixteen, and that I can play the piano, speak six languages fluently, and I'm an ex-model, so I know a lot about fashion and poise. I can fly a plane, ride a motorcycle and shoot very well. I also like camping. I think I have a lot going for me and can hold my own."

He of all people didn't need to be told about her many skills and attributes. He knew them well. The one he didn't know about was her skill in the bedroom. That was the only one he was interested in right now.

"Of course, you can hold your own, Regan. All I'm saying is that most men who use that dating service might be looking for a wife, but they aren't looking for love. Are you willing to marry someone who doesn't love you?"

"I would think any man is capable of falling in love if the right woman came along, Garth. Except for you, and you've explained your reasons. Any man of wealth and influence has access to a variety of women if all they want to do is date or take care of their physical needs. A man using that caliber of dating service is looking for more and that's what I want, too. Just because you're not looking for love in a marriage doesn't mean every man who uses that dating service feels the same way."

She had a point there. Other men might not have an aversion to falling in love with the woman the dating service selected for them. There was no doubt in his mind that any man who chose Regan would be wowed by her. She was beautiful and accomplished. He could see any man falling in love with her.

"So when we return to Fairbanks, I'd like the information for the service so I can contact them before the holidays."

He pushed his plate aside, trying to hide his annoyance. "Why the rush?"

"No rush. I just figure that like most companies, they will have limited hours around the holidays. If I get my information in now, maybe by early spring I will have viable prospects. I will be twenty-nine by then.

It would be nice to have someone special to celebrate my birthday with."

For some reason he felt a chill at the thought of her spending her birthday with anyone other than his family, like she had this year. Since Franklin had moved to Florida, Charm had known it would be Regan's first birthday without her father, so Charm had hosted a dinner party in Regan's honor at the Outlaw Estates. Even Bart had joined them.

"I'll make sure you get the information when we return to Alaska."

She smiled over at him. "Thank you, Garth."

Why did she have to sound so happy about it, and why did he feel like a selfish ass again? He wanted to have an affair with her with no promises of a future, but he was getting annoyed that she wanted to meet someone who could give her the love he couldn't.

He pushed the negatives to the back of his mind and decided to concentrate on the positives. Right now, the main positive was that she'd agreed to have an affair with him.

"What are your plans today?" he asked.

She shrugged. "It's too late to go hiking, so what do you suggest?"

He would suggest they head straight to the nearest bedroom, but as much as he desired her, he wanted her to decide when they would become intimate. "Whatever you want to do is fine with me. I told Paulo that he didn't have to return for the rest of the day. That means I'll be doing all the cooking today," he said.

"I'll help," she said as she stood to take their plates.

He watched as she walked over to the counter, loving the way her knit sweater fit over her leggings and across her backside. After placing the dishes in the sink, she turned and caught him staring again.

A smile touched the corners of her lips. "I just thought of something I'd like to do today."

"You did?" he asked in a voice that sounded almost too deep to be his own.

"Yes."

Their gazes held for a long moment. "What?" he finally asked.

"Come here and I'll tell you."

Garth heard a sexy catch in her voice, and it did something to him. Had him pushing his chair back to stand and cross the room to her. "Yes?"

"Move closer, Garth."

He could do that, and he did. A second later he was standing so close their bodies were touching. He could actually feel her nipples poking into his chest. "Yes?"

"Today I want to feel sexy, desired and wanted. Do you think you can handle that, Garth?"

Sexy, desired and wanted...

Images of how he could make her feel those very things spiked through his brain. "I know I can handle it, Regan."

She reached up and placed her arms around his neck. Tilting her head back, she looked up at him. "Then show me."

Fourteen

Garth drew her into his arms, lowered his head and kissed her. The moment their mouths touched, Regan knew she had made the right decision. This was what she wanted. Closing her eyes, she intended to get the full, unadulterated effect.

This was what she needed, and she hadn't known just how much until now. Seeing him walk toward her in those jeans and that T-shirt had made every hormone in her body burn. Seeing how the denim stretched across a pair of muscled thighs and how his broad chest and brawny shoulders were killing that T-shirt had made her heart flutter deep in her chest.

This kiss was different from the one they'd shared last night. It was passionate, but there was something else, too. It was seductive, fiery to the point where she moaned as their tongues mingled. Heat spread all through her body.

Garth's mouth was a perfect fit over hers. She'd noticed that last night and noticed it again today. His kiss drugged all her senses and made her want more, more and more. When he deepened the kiss, her moans deepened, as well.

He wanted her. She had the ability to taste the depth of his desire in the onslaught of his greedy mouth. Was it intentional? Was he deliberately letting her know his desire for her hadn't changed? Was that why he was greedily lapping up her mouth, making her aware of his voraciousness? His insatiability?

She groaned in protest when he finally ended the kiss, but not before he used the tip of his tongue to lick her mouth from corner to corner. Opening her eyes, she gazed up into his dark brown ones while drawing in a deep breath. She loved him so much. He had no idea that she loved him. He thought all he wanted from her was sex, but she intended to make things so good between them that in the end he would think twice about letting her go build a future with another man. She was taking a gamble with her plan, but he was worth the risk.

"Are you sure about this, Regan?" he asked. "If you say yes, just know that before we return to Fairbanks, I intend to make love to you all over this house."

The thought had sizzling sensations spreading between her legs. If his words were meant to be a reality check for her, they had been. She was all too eager to mix her fantasies with his reality to see what they came up with. Her goal was to make him desire her more than he did now, more than he ever thought he could.

"I'm sure, but what about you, Garth? Are you sure, as well?"

"Sweetheart, I've never been so sure of anything before in my life."

He then swept her off her feet and into his arms and began moving. She knew he was taking her to a bedroom, and she didn't care which one. It didn't matter. Either would work.

Regan knew the moment he placed her on the bed that they were in the bedroom he'd slept in last night. His manly scent was all over the bedcovers. It aroused her. Made her feel as if her entire body was burning alive from the inside out.

"May I go on record to make something clear, Regan?" Garth asked, kicking off his shoes.

She swallowed. He was standing, all six feet and three inches of him, at the foot of the bed, staring at her with the same intensity that she felt. She wasn't sure what he had to say, but she definitely wanted to hear it.

"Yes," she said in an almost whisper.

"You don't need me to make you feel sexy, desired and wanted. You are those things already. What I intend to do is to make you feel needed," he said, stepping away from the bed to pull his T-shirt over his head and toss it on a nearby chair. "If only you knew the depth of my need for you."

She wondered if being needed also meant she was indispensable, essential, vital, crucial…all those things she wanted to become to him.

"Now I have you just where I want you, Regan. In my bed."

And whether he knew it or not, she had him just where she wanted him, too. Standing in front of her and stripping, for starters. As she watched, his hands went to the front of his jeans.

"And I have you doing what I've always fantasized about, Garth. Taking your clothes off in front of me so I can see you naked."

She could tell from the look on his face that her words surprised him. "You used to fantasize about me?"

"All the time. You always looked sexy in your business suits, but my imagination gets a little more risqué than that."

He shook his head. "I never knew."

"What? That I wanted you as much as you wanted me? I told you that in the kitchen earlier."

"I assumed that desire began since you've been here with me."

Boy, was he wrong. "No, it goes back further than that."

It was important that he knew everything. Not only that the desire was mutual but also that it hadn't just begun. If he understood that then it would be easier for her to build the kind of relationship they needed, regardless of whether he thought they needed it or not.

"I never knew," he said, looking a little confused. "You never said anything."

"I wasn't supposed to. You are my boss and I am a professional."

He nodded because she knew he couldn't refute that. "How long have you felt that way?"

There was no way she would tell him that she'd had a crush on him since she was sixteen, or that he was the reason she had returned to Fairbanks after her first year in college. She had heard he was back home from the military with a broken heart, and she'd been determined to fix it. Things didn't work out quite that way. He was deep in mourning for the woman he'd lost and had built a solid wall around himself, one that even his family hadn't been able to penetrate for a long while.

"The length of time doesn't matter, Garth. All you need to know is that the desire between us is mutual. Now are you going to finish undressing or what?"

He gave her that Garth Outlaw smile, and her gaze shifted lower, from his face to where his hand rested at his zipper. He was fully aroused. That much was obvious. Seeing him had the tips of her breasts responding.

Her heart raced in her chest and she couldn't recall another time when seeing a half-naked man had done that to her. But she knew it was more than seeing Garth without his shirt, because he'd been bare-chested around her before. It was Garth, period.

The man she had truly loved forever.

Her gaze was fixated on his zipper and it was quite obvious that he was aware it wasn't his zipper per se that held her interest. "Are you ready for me, Regan?"

She was ready for him, and ready to see him. "I am ready for you, Garth."

"Do you want to touch me now?" he invited, tapping his crotch.

She swallowed. That invitation was bold, and it made the tips of her fingers itch. She glanced up and met his gaze. "Copping a feel won't satisfy me. I'd rather touch you there when you're not wearing any clothes."

She saw the flare of heat in his eyes and smiled. Little did he know she intended to touch him—and taste him—all over. By the time they left for Fairbanks, she hoped he would have become so addicted to her touch that he would seek her out to continue what they'd started here.

"I'm not one to keep a lady waiting."

Her eyes were glued to his crotch when he began lowering his zipper. When he slid the jeans down muscled thighs and legs, her breath caught. The only thing left was his briefs and they were barely keeping him contained. She watched as he lowered them down his legs.

"Wow," she said, with both awe and feminine appreciation in her voice.

He smiled over at her. "Now are you ready to touch me?"

Garth knew that for as long as he lived, he would never forget the look on Regan's face the moment she saw him totally naked. She had no idea how much her expression boosted his ego. And he wasn't a man whose ego needed stroking. However, he was discovering that when it came to Regan, she got to him in a way that wasn't normal.

He'd been attracted to beautiful women before, but for some reason his attraction to her was different. For months, he'd tried to downplay it. Then he'd gone through a period of denial because there was no reason for him to all of a sudden become fixated on her. When ignoring it didn't work, he'd accepted his attraction to her was only physical. After sex, he thought, he would get back to normal. Once he'd gotten his fill of her—worked her out of his system while they spent time together here in Santa Cruz—then things between them would get back to normal when they returned to Fairbanks.

And for her to admit she'd wanted him long before now made desiring her even more acceptable to him. He didn't have to feel guilty about seducing her when she'd let it be known she wanted to be seduced. Just to think, they'd had the hots for each other, but had kept it secret. Imagine all the times he had wanted her and could have had her.

"Yes, I want to touch you, but shouldn't I take my clothes off, too?" she asked.

He nodded. "That might be a good idea because when you touch me, I'm going to want to touch you."

She grinned over at him. "Please do."

He'd been so used to the very professional, highly proficient Regan Fairchild that he'd have to adjust to the sexy woman reclining on that bed.

She eased up and pulled her top over her head and tossed it to join his T-shirt on the chair. Next came her black lace bra. She was taking her time unhooking it and he felt a stirring deep in the pit of his stomach as he watched her. Feeling a little impatient, he asked, "Need help?"

She shook her head. "No, I've got this."

When she removed her bra and tossed it aside to expose a pair of gorgeous breasts with delicious-looking, darkened nipples, his tongue tightened in this mouth.

"Now for these," she said, working the leggings down her thighs. That left her clad in a pair of scanty, black lace panties.

"May I?" he asked.

She glanced over at him. "May you do what?"

"Take those off you?"

He watched how she drew in a deep breath as if his question had affected her. "If you want," she said. To him the sound of her voice was breathlessly husky.

"Yes, I want." Garth doubted she knew just how much he wanted.

He moved toward the bed and thought the same thing now that he'd thought when he'd seen her in her swimsuit. She had a gorgeous body. Seeing her small waist, flat tummy and a pair of long, beautiful legs made breathing difficult.

He felt heat in the tips of his fingers when he placed them beneath the waistband of her panties. He heard her sharp intake of breath when he touched her skin. When he slowly began easing the panties down her legs, anticipation took over his senses.

When he had uncovered her, Garth went completely still. He'd never seen anything so beautiful. Something passed through him, something akin to possession, which didn't make sense. They weren't in an exclusive relationship. All they would be sharing was an affair that would last only while they were here in Santa Cruz. Why did he need to remind himself of that?

"Garth?"

He shifted his gaze from her feminine mound to her face. "Who will do the touching first?"

He swallowed. The hell with touching, he wanted to taste her, but she might not be ready for that yet, so he said. "Ladies first."

She evidently liked his answer. She crawled toward him and took him into her hands and cupped him. He knew he was a goner. "Not sure I'm going to last, Regan," he said, gritting his teeth to keep from groaning aloud when she worked her fingers on him.

Deciding he needed to touch her while she was touching him, he took her breasts in his hands, loving the way they felt. Then he leaned forward and sucked a hardened nipple between his lips.

"Garth!"

He released her breast as she released him. "I need you, Regan."

"And I need you. Now."

An aura of sexual chemistry surrounded them. He'd known for almost a year that he wanted her, but he hadn't expected to need her to this degree. Reaching over, he reached into the nightstand to retrieve a condom packet. He quickly ripped it open and sheathed himself, knowing she watched his every move.

Then, joining her on the bed, he straddled his body over hers. Her feminine scent fueled his desire. It had blood rushing fast and furious through his veins, causing a spike of heat to rush into his groin. Anticipation thickened the air and he bit back a guttural groan.

Leaning in, he captured her mouth with his, needing to taste her. When he couldn't wait any longer, he eased his engorged shaft inside of her, feeling how her body stretched for him. Glancing down, he saw the glassy look in her eyes, and when she whispered, "Deeper," he thrust hard, filling her totally and completely.

Garth gazed down at her and found her staring up at him. He loved the feel of being inside her, how her inner muscles clenched him. How her fingernails dug into his shoulders. He began moving, thrusting back and forth, and she extracted everything out of him.

Over and over he pounded into her, establishing a rhythm, a sensuous beat, that he could move to forever. He was taking her hard, fast and then harder and faster, not letting up. He needed this. He wanted her. He needed her.

The sound of her moaning and then purring and then moaning again pushed him over the edge. Throwing his head back, he continued to thrust hard, trying to go deeper with every stroke while loving the feel of her inner muscles clenching him even tighter.

Suddenly, he released a loud growl, one he was certain shook the rafters. But he couldn't stop. Wasn't sure if he would ever stop. His body bucked and she screamed out her pleasure. Every inch of him was filling her. Just the way he wanted. Just the way he'd dreamed. Never had he shared an orgasm with a woman who had rocked him all the way to the bone.

Her muscles continued to grip him, to pull everything out of him as he thrust hard, heading toward another climax right on the heels of the first. Then, when he knew he had nothing left to give, he collapsed on top of her before quickly shifting so his weight would not harm her.

"Regan."

"Garth."

Somehow, he found enough energy to kiss her again. What they'd shared wasn't ordinary. It was something he hadn't counted on. When had he ever desired a woman this much? Even now he felt himself getting aroused all over again.

Releasing her mouth, he eased out of bed to take care of the condom. "I'll be back in a minute and when I return…"

She glanced up at him with satisfied eyes. "Yes?"

"I intend to taste you all over."

Fifteen

Regan forced her eyes open and looked up at Garth. He had more energy than he knew what to do with. Well, that wasn't totally true since he did know what to do with it. He did her. Over and over again. Not once, or twice, not even three times. They had been going at it since breakfast, skipping lunch and napping in between. And when he'd told her he would taste her all over, he'd meant it. No man had ever done anything like that to her before. Making love to Garth had definitely been an adventure.

"No way we haven't worked up an appetite. It's time for me to get up and fix dinner since we skipped lunch," Garth said, easing his body off her and pulling her into his arms.

"Not sure I'll make dinner," she said. All she felt like

doing was sleeping and burying her face in the bedcovers that smelled like him. The scent of a man. A robust man. A very sexual man. A man who had more stamina than the law allowed. But he'd also been tender and caring. He hadn't done anything without first making sure she was comfortable with it. Everything he'd done had filled her with pleasure, pleasure and more pleasure.

"You have to eat, Regan," he said, leaning down and placing a kiss on her lips.

She loved it whenever he kissed her, and he'd been kissing her a lot today. All over. "Why? So you can zap away all my strength and energy again?"

He grinned. "Did I do that?"

"Yes. And you don't have to look so pleased about it." And he was looking pleased. She'd seen Garth smile a lot of times, but this was a different kind of smile. One that showed an unusual side of him. A sensual side. A side that openly displayed emotions she hadn't seen him expose in a long time. Not since he'd returned from the military.

"Hard not to look pleased when I am. Not about zapping your energy or strength, but the fact that I'm here and you're here with me."

"News flash, Mr. Outlaw. I'm usually with you," she reminded him. Hopefully, to give him something to think about. "You've been doing a lot of traveling lately and I'm your transportation in the air and often on the ground."

"I like this way better. With you in bed with me."

She knew that for now, it was all sexual for him. She could deal with that as long as she believed there could be more down the road. "I guess I should get up and help you with dinner."

"You don't have to. I like taking care of you for a change. You're always taking care of me. Like you just said, whether it's in the air or on the ground, you're my girl."

She bit back the temptation of telling him that she wanted to be more than *his girl*. She wanted to be his wife, and she hoped one day he realized that she could be everything he needed. "Thanks. But staying in bed will make me lazy."

He smiled. "I doubt you know the meaning of the word, and if you do feel like slacking off, that's fine because you deserve it. Besides, you are on vacation."

"I've never helped you cook before," she said. "I want to do it."

"Suit yourself," he said, easing out of bed. Then as if he thought better of it, he leaned back on his haunches and threw the bed covers off her.

"Hey! What do you think you're doing?"

He grinned. "I just want to see you naked again," he said as his gaze roamed all over her. "You want to try out the hot tub after dinner?"

"Sure. Sounds like it will be fun."

"Trust me, sweetheart. I intend to make it fun."

"Grab that measuring cup over there for me please, Regan."

"Sure thing. But why don't you just estimate? That's the way Dad does it."

Garth was trying to keep his attention on what he

was making and not on Regan, who was acting as his assistant. The distraction wouldn't be so bad if she wasn't wearing his T-shirt and nothing else. And he knew for a fact she was completely bare beneath it. No panties. No bra. Nothing but the most delectable and soft skin imaginable.

"Roberta was a stickler and felt everything had to be measured, and that's how she taught me. On the other hand, Franklin is such a whiz at everything he does. He could probably prepare a delicious five-course meal with his eyes closed."

Regan smiled. "Yes, Dad could probably do that. While growing up, whenever he left on a trip, he would prepare enough food for me to eat while he was gone." She chuckled. "He would even date the containers so I would know what to eat and when."

"Wasn't there someone staying with you while he was gone?"

"Yes, Ms. Petry. She was a good housekeeper, but couldn't cook worth a darn. I complained to Dad, but he thought I was being overly critical. At least he thought that until he ate some of the food himself. Since she was good at everything else, he didn't want to let her go. Besides, he liked knowing I was eating healthy."

Garth knew that Franklin had enlisted in the air force in his twenties, where he was a cook for a while. Four years later, when it was time to reenlist, he'd expressed his desire to become a pilot and was granted his request. What would Franklin think of the proposition Garth had made to his daughter? More than once Franklin had told him that Regan was no longer a child but an adult who was mature enough to make any decisions governing her life. Garth was glad Franklin felt that way, because her decision to have an affair with Garth had been hers to make.

He had a feeling his siblings wouldn't be as accepting of it if they knew. His brothers, on more their one occasion, had appointed themselves Regan's guard dogs. Especially Sloan and Maverick. For that reason, although they were aware Regan was here with him, he wanted to be sure they had no idea Garth and Regan had become lovers. It was a good thing their affair would end when they left here. Otherwise, there was no doubt in his mind his brothers would have a lot to say about something that was none of their business.

"Here you are."

He turned and accepted the measuring cup from Regan. The moment their hands touched, intense heat curled inside his gut. She'd been eager to help him with dinner, and he appreciated her enthusiasm. However, she had no idea what being around her in a T-shirt that barely covered her thighs was doing to him. Watching her swish around in the kitchen aroused him all over again. After finally leaving the bed, they had showered together, which had been something dreams were made of. If he wasn't careful, he could become addicted to all this passion, and this was just day one.

"Thanks."

"You're welcome.

Brownies were his specialty and one of the easiest things to bake—if he could just concentrate on making them. Instead, every time Regan moved, his gaze moved with her. He was trying really hard to retain his sanity, by telling himself he'd seen a pair of nice-looking thighs a lot of times. But his subconscious would counter: *never Regan's and never this much.* They just reminded him how it had felt being between those thighs.

"Will it be much longer?"

He glanced over at her. She stood close to him and he inhaled her scent. Shower-fresh, clean and jasmine. "Not too much longer. The baked chicken will be ready to come out of the oven about the same time I'll be ready to slide this batch of brownies in." He'd decided to bake brownies because he knew just how much Regan liked them. Now she would get a chance to try his.

A half hour later, he took off his apron. The baked chicken and rice pilaf were done, the broccoli and carrots were simmering and the brownies were in the oven. He glanced over at Regan. "Thanks. You were a big help."

She laughed. "I did my best. Are you sure I didn't get in the way?"

"No, you didn't get in the way." He glanced at his watch. "We have a little less than an hour before everything will be ready."

"Do you want to go for a walk?" she asked him.

He pulled her close and rubbed his hand down her arms. He loved seeing her body's reaction to his touch. They didn't have time for a full-blown lovemaking session and he'd never been one for quickies. For him, lovemaking was something to be savored, appreciated and made to last as long as it could.

"We can take a walk after dinner. I prefer doing

something else." He saw the way her eyes immediately darkened and knew what she assumed he was about to suggest. "Not that, either. I'm looking forward to tonight."

"Oh? Then what?"

Was that disappointment he heard in her voice? His hands slid from her arms to her waist. "You ever played a kissing game?"

She lifted a brow. "Kissing game? Can't say that I have. Have you?"

He shook his head, grinning. "No, but when I was in the Marines, it was a game the guys would talk about. Evidently, it's a popular game that the Lower 48 are used to playing, but me and Walker, the only ones from Alaska, had never heard of it."

"How is it played?"

"For starters, like this." Pulling her to him, he leaned down and captured her mouth in his. On her moan, his tongue slid inside her mouth. He loved the way her body automatically responded to him, whether to lovemaking or kisses.

He deepened the kiss, and she reciprocated. Their mouths mated greedily, voraciously. For a moment, he felt as if he could eat her alive. He had allowed his body to go without sex for a while. What would she think if she knew he hadn't made love to a woman since the Westmorelands' charity ball?

He released her mouth. She was panting, but then so was he. Every time he kissed her, desire twisted his guts. Maybe he should back out of this kissing game.

He might not be able to stand the heat that would be generated.

Sweeping her off her feet and into his arms, he left the kitchen and walked to the living room. He eased down onto the sofa with her in his arms, his hand coming into contact with her bare bottom.

"So, what's this kissing game called, Garth?"

One of the things he liked about her was that she didn't have an aversion to trying something different. "Too Hot."

She nodded while adjusting her body to sit up in his lap. There was no way she wasn't aware of his aroused state. "How is it played?'

Just looking at her made him want to bury his face in the hollow of her throat to breathe in her scent. He was still that attracted to her. Making love hadn't even put a dent in his desire. She was still very much in his system, and he wasn't sure how he was going to get her out of there. But he had to do it by the time they left here. He had no choice.

"The object of the game is for a couple to kiss without stopping and without touching each other. If one of the players touches the other in any way, then he or she loses and the winner gets to do whatever he or she wants to the loser."

He saw the lifting of her brow and knew she had questions. "Yes?"

"What if I really need to breathe? I'm not good at holding my breath for a long period of time."

"All you have to do is break off the kiss, but you only get a couple of seconds to suck in air."

She frowned. "A couple of seconds?"

"Yes. I'm being generous."

"You really think so?" she asked him, looking none too sure of that.

He chuckled. "Okay, take no more than five seconds. I am modifying the rules, but if you don't think you can stand the heat then stay out of the kitchen."

"Oh, I plan on getting you so hot, Garth, steam will be coming out of your ears. There's no way you won't lose."

Sliding her off his lap, he placed her on the sofa beside him and turned to face her. "Bring it on, Regan."

Kissing but no touching…

Regan was convinced whoever had thought of this kissing game needed to have their head examined, and she needed hers checked just for agreeing to play. But she would find any excuse to kiss Garth—the kicker would be not touching him. She liked rubbing her hands over his chest whenever his tongue was inside her mouth. Earlier, she'd even cupped him a few times and loved touching him there.

"Ready to start?" She looked at Garth, saw the dark heat in his eyes. He was so sure of his abilities that he'd basically already declared himself the winner. It was there in his gaze and the smile curving his lips. Well, she would have to show him.

More than anything, she had to stay in control of her senses. All five of them. Taste wasn't off the table because that was the main sense they would be using. Since touching was off the table, it would be the biggest temptation. Closing her eyes would take care of her sense of sight, but she wasn't sure about the hearing and smell. Just hearing him groan did things to her and he had a scent that turned her on.

"Regan?"

Drawing in a deep breath and forcing her hands to her side, she nodded. "Yes, let's do this."

Not waiting for him, she leaned in and went straight for his luscious mouth.

Sixteen

Mercy! Regan had charged into his mouth like her life depended on it. The action had surprised him so much that he had to remember where they were and what they were doing. On instinct he'd almost reached out to lock his arms around her, but then caught himself. Touching her was the one thing he couldn't do.

He had to calm his pounding heart and take charge of the situation. She'd gotten a head start and he'd been swept up in how she made him feel. Explosive sensations had settled right in his groin. Once he took control, he figured it would all be over. Already he was thinking about what he would have her do when she lost.

He returned her kiss with an urgency he felt in every part of his body. Deepening the kiss, he whipped his tongue from her grasp and became the aggressor. He knew he had succeeded when he felt her move under his mouth. He nearly lost it when he heard her moan. He balled his hands into fists at his side. Otherwise, he would be tempted to use those hands to stroke her all over, to slide them underneath that T-shirt and caress her breasts. Garth didn't want to stop there.

She suddenly snatched her mouth away to draw in a breath and then she was back at it, reclaiming his mouth as if determined to regain command. And for a moment she did. Regan had caught him off guard when she broke off the kiss. In those quick three seconds, he'd been focused on the sight of her wet lips, and now she'd gotten the upper hand. This was a full-contact, wet-tongued, bone-melting kind of kiss.

He was fighting like hell to get back his mastery but discovered it wasn't as easy as he'd thought it would be. She was kissing him in a way that spilled intense pleasure within his very soul. It was if this was a kiss of intent. One of possession.

Never had a woman kissed him like this before. A part of him suspected she'd never kissed a man like this before, either. She wasn't behaving like an experienced kisser, but like one who'd discovered something new that she liked. She was getting all she could out of it.

Damn. What had he created?

That question was lost on him when she used deep, hot glides of her tongue in his mouth, silently demanding that he return the favor, so he did. Then she sucked on it in a way that made his erection throb.

He knew what he wanted. Here and now. He wanted to take this kiss to a whole other level. He wanted more of her taste. He wanted all he could get. In every way that he could get it.

When she moved to take his mouth again, he tumbled her back on the sofa.

He could tell by her expression that she hadn't expected that maneuver. "You touched me. Garth."

That wasn't all he was about to do to her.

"I'm hot. I'll worry about all the steam coming out of my ears later, Regan."

Standing, he quickly pulled the shirt over his head and shoved the jeans down his legs. Regan was on her back with the T-shirt pulled up above her hips, her legs spread. He couldn't have dreamed a better pose.

"I want to kiss you there, Regan," he said, getting out of his briefs.

"That involves touching. Are you forfeiting the game?"

He grinned. She could honestly worry about the outcome of the game at a time like this? But then maybe he was the only one sexually riled to the point of losing control. Had he misinterpreted her arousing scent? Hell, he didn't think so.

"May I kiss you there?" he asked her, to make sure they were on the same page.

"You're forfeiting the game?"

Whatever it took. "Yes," he said, practically licking his lips.

"Then, yes. You may kiss me down there all you want."

Quickly dropping to his knees in front of her, he buried his head between her legs.

* * *

You may kiss me down there all you want…

"Ohhh," Regan moaned and wondered how she could have possibly told Garth something like that. Hadn't he proved that morning just what a naughty mouth he had? And just what wickedly sensuous things he was capable of doing with his tongue?

She couldn't believe all the attention he was giving to her. Right there. He was paying her back for all those things she'd done to his mouth while kissing him. Now he was doing them to her—there. He was making it nearly impossible to keep still. That was why her hips were moving and why he'd clamped down on them firmly with his hands to keep them steady. She was practically locked under his mouth.

Regan was dying of pleasure, she was sure of it. She bit down on her bottom lip to keep from screaming. Never had so many erotic points seized her senses all at once. She was tossed in a state of sexual frenzy, causing her to rock her body against his mouth.

He retaliated by sinking his tongue even deeper inside of her, pushing her over the edge. Unable to take this much pleasure any longer, she screamed his name when her body jerked into a shattering climax that seemed to go on forever.

The intensity of her orgasm brought tears to her eyes. She was still whimpering in pleasure when his body moved to straddle hers. Opening her eyes, she saw Garth, right there. Their gazes held and he kissed her tears away.

Such unexpected tenderness made her want to cry

even more. Instead, she wrapped her arms around his neck and guided his mouth to hers. They kissed with a greed that renewed her desire for him, made her fall deeper in love with him.

He released her mouth and stared down at her. The desire in his eyes caused heat to reignite between her legs. As if he felt it, too, he entered her, fitting snugly in the vee of her thighs. He began moving, setting the rhythm while staring down at her. She was too transfixed to look away.

She watched as his brows drew together as if some thought had suddenly entered his mind. She knew what it was.

"I'm on the pill, Garth."

His brows relaxed. Leaning in, he kissed her. The moment his mouth touched hers, a climax rushed through her. It seemed hers triggered his own. Cupping a hand beneath her bottom, he tilted her hips then moaned inside her mouth when pleasure took him over.

No sooner had their bodies relaxed than the oven's buzzer went off. They had done all of that in fifty minutes? Amazing. When he eased off her, he pulled her up to a sitting position beside him. Instinctively, her body curled into him. At that moment she doubted if she'd ever felt more content.

Hours later, Garth entered his bedroom to change clothes. He would be rejoining Regan in fifteen minutes to enjoy the hot tub. Dinner had been awesome, if he did say so himself. Regan had said so, too. She'd gone on and on about how delicious it was. He'd been quick to remind her that they had prepared the meal together and that she'd been an excellent helper.

He hadn't been giving her any BS, because she had been a great assistant. He had enjoyed having her there with him, sharing his space. She was the first woman to ever do so. There was never a time that he and Karen had shared kitchen duties. Nor had they ever played any kissing games. And he'd never gotten the chance to perform oral sex on her. Hell, he wasn't sure if she would have liked it. He did recall that the few times they had made love, she'd gotten up immediately afterward, saying she wasn't the cuddling type. He'd gotten used to that.

Regan, however, was the cuddling type, and now he was getting used to how she liked things. Either way was fine with him, but he found Regan's way of wanting to be held afterward a lot more intimate.

He inhaled a deep breath as he began stripping off his clothes to change into his swimming shorts. He couldn't stop thinking of that kissing contest. Boy, had he enjoyed it, from start to finish. Of course, it hadn't finished the way it should have, but he had no complaints…other than one. Since he'd forfeited the game, that made her the winner. That meant she could do whatever she wanted with him. He couldn't help wondering what she had in mind.

Garth had finished changing when his cell phone went off. He recognized the caller as Maverick and was surprised his youngest brother had waited this long to call. Maverick had a tendency to make a pest of himself, but deep down Garth knew he wouldn't have it any other way. Maverick was Maverick.

He grabbed the phone off his bed. "What's going on with you, Maverick?"

"I should be asking that of you. Are you treating my girl right?"

His girl? "If you're referring to Regan, yes, I'm the perfect host."

"Good. She needs to enjoy herself. Working for you isn't easy, Garth. You're demanding. Too serious at times. Too driven. Hanging around you for any period of time can be stressful. You work too hard. Regan deserves time to enjoy herself. To chill. I just hope like hell that you're not boring her."

Garth smiled when he thought of what all he and Regan had done that day. He could safely say she wasn't at all bored. The sound of her screaming out her pleasure was still ringing in his ears.

"Look, Mav, I need to go take a shower," he lied.

"Okay, and tell Regan I said hello."

"I will. Talk to you later."

He clicked off the phone and quickly left the bedroom. He didn't want to keep Regan waiting.

Seventeen

The next morning, Regan slowly opened her eyes. The first thing she noted was that she was in bed alone. How had Garth left without waking her? When she had drifted off to sleep last night, he'd been holding her in his arms, with their limbs entwined. She must have been sleeping pretty hard not to have felt him disengaging their bodies.

She glanced at the clock on Garth's nightstand as the aroma of bacon flowed through her nostrils. It was breakfast time and Paulo was back. But she would have to say, Garth had done a great job at breakfast yesterday. In her book, Garth had done a great job in everything yesterday.

Dinner had been great and the brownies had been delicious. To top everything off, their lovemaking had been wonderful. Both before and after dinner. When she thought about what all they'd done in that hot tub, she couldn't help but blush. And then last night, right here in this bedroom. They'd taken another shower together— their second that day—and then he'd dried her off, swept her into his arms and carried her to his bed to make love to her again.

She'd made love more times in one day and night than she'd done in the past three years. The mere thought had her pulse racing, mainly because it hadn't been with just anyone, but with the man she loved.

She eased up in bed, wondering where Garth had gone and why he hadn't awakened her before leaving. Did Paulo know they were sharing a bed? Did she care? No, she didn't, because she was an adult and free to do as she pleased. The same held true for Garth.

Even so, she had a feeling Garth wouldn't be mentioning their affair to anyone. At least that was the feeling she'd gotten when he mentioned last night in the hot tub that Maverick had called and sent his regards. There was no way Garth would have given Maverick a hint the two of them had something going on. If he had, Maverick would have called her, probably to try talking her out of it.

More than once, he had warned her about guys who meant her no good. She was the marrying kind and should never, ever settle for anything less. He would definitely see any affair with his oldest brother as settling. Especially if he discovered Garth had warned her he could never fall in love with her. Maverick, like everyone in their family, knew Garth was still in love with

Karen. Maverick would never understand that although she knew it, too, she was hoping that Garth would see over the next two weeks that she was wife material as much as any other woman.

She wanted him to enjoy their time together so much he would be willing to take a chance on them as a couple. She knew it was a risk, but she didn't care. Some risks were worth taking.

"Whatever you're thinking about must be serious."

She glanced over to the doorway and smiled when she saw Garth leaning there. Why did have to look so jaw-droppingly gorgeous standing there shirtless, with his jeans riding low on his hips?

"Good morning. I was just thinking about Dad," she lied. There was no way she could tell Garth what she was really thinking about.

The smile disappeared from his face and he came into the room to stand beside the bed. "Why? Is something wrong with Franklin?"

She heard the panic in his voice and understood. He had a close relationship with her father, and she had been surprised he hadn't used that relationship as a reason for him not having an affair with her. She was glad that Garth had believed her father all those times he'd said he accepted Regan as the adult she was. Her father knew that if she made mistakes along the way, she would learn from them. Now she was beginning to wonder if loving Garth as much as she did would be a mistake she would eventually learn from. Her main question to herself was, if that was the case, would it be one she would recover from?

Franklin Fairchild believed that, like him, his daughter was a fighter. He had encountered the biggest fight of his life when he'd moved on with his daughter after unexpectedly losing the wife he adored. He had moved on without another woman to love.

Would Garth be like her father?

"Yes, Dad is fine. He should be returning from his cruise in a few days. He's had his cell phone off and I don't expect him to turn it back on until he reaches one of the islands that are part of the United States territories."

He nodded and she could see his features relax. "I'm glad he's enjoying his life."

"Yes, but I wish he could enjoy it more."

"How so?" He came to sit on the edge of the bed and—as if it were the most natural thing—he reached out and took her hand in his. An electric current pulsed where he touched.

"There were times when I would walk into a room and he would be just sitting there staring at Mom's picture. Those were the times when I knew his heart was in pain. He loved her so much that he refused to move on. Dad's a very handsome man, and a number of women made it known they would have loved for him to return their interest. But he didn't. He dated on occasion, but he pretty much decided that only one woman could have his heart."

Garth didn't say anything, and she knew why. He and her father shared the same views in that respect.

Maybe this would be a good time for them to talk about it again. A couple of days ago he'd told her he could never love another woman, but she wanted to believe his heart was big enough to share. Why, like her father, did he not believe that?

"I know where Franklin is coming from, Regan. It's not easy to fall in love a second time when your heart is still consumed with memories of the first. I recall the number of times Franklin would say you helped keep Geneva's memory alive because you looked so much like her. And you had her spirit and compassion. I agree. Geneva was a beautiful woman. I recall when she began working for the company and how smitten Franklin was of her. I was a kid and I walked in on them kissing once."

Her eyes widened. "You did?"

He chuckled. "Yes. However, before your mind gets overloaded with scandalous thoughts, they were married, but you hadn't been born yet. On that particular day, he'd flown my dad on a business trip somewhere in the Lower 48 and had been gone for at least two weeks. Roberta took all of us out to meet the plane when it returned. Geneva was there waiting, too."

He paused. "Your dad always looked dapper in his uniform, and being the professional that he was, he waited until he'd taken care of all the paperwork before he got off the plane. Your mom waited patiently. I remember having to go to the bathroom. I went down some hallway near one of the hangars and he and your mom were there. I guess you could say they were letting each other know how much they were missed."

"Ah, how romantic," she said, imagining the scene.

He looked over at her and smiled. "And if I do recall, nine months later you were born."

Regan threw her head back and laughed. She laughed a lot around him and she noticed he laughed a lot around her. She loved how he would share these fond memories with her.

Now she needed to ask him something that would place a damper on the mood, but she needed to know.

"Garth?"

"Yes, sweetheart?"

That was the second time he'd referred to her that way, and yes, she was keeping count. She doubted he was aware that whenever he used that term of endearment it made her heart swell. "Tell me about her."

He lifted a brow. "Who? Your mom?"

She shook her head. "No. About Karen."

For a long moment, he didn't say anything, and just stared at her. Then he slowly released her hand and stood. "Why do you want to know anything about Karen? I told you all you needed to know about her, which was that I love her and will always love her. What else is there for you to know?"

Regan nervously nibbled her bottom lip. She could give him a page of reasons, but none that she could tell him without putting him on the defense. Why was he hesitating? Her father would have seized on any opportunity to talk about her mother. A part of Regan didn't understand why Garth wouldn't do the same. Granted, any information about Karen wasn't her business, but a part of her wanted to know.

She shrugged her shoulders. "I just want to know

about the woman who still has your heart. I think that's a special kind of love."

He didn't say anything for a minute and then he walked over to the dresser and leaned against it, as if he needed to put distance between them. Six feet of distance. He drew in a deep breath and said, "I don't think I will ever forget the first time I saw her. Walker and I went into a club on base and there she was, sitting at a table with friends, other female soldiers.

"I could tell she seemed nervous about being in the club. After I met her, I found out why. Her parents were very religious. Her father had been a minister. It was obvious she wasn't used to being in such a place. Guilt was written all over her face."

He rubbed his hand down his face and Regan knew reliving the memories was hard on him. "When we began dating, I would take her to nice places off base. The zoo, various museums and markets. Then we got our orders to leave and discovered we were headed for the same place in Syria. By then, we'd been dating exclusively for four months. I knew we were head over heels in love with each other. We talked about marriage. I'd even met her parents and her older brother when we had chance to go visit while on leave. Unfortunately, she never got to travel to Alaska to meet my family."

He paused a moment and she could see deep sadness in his eyes when he finally said, "I will never forget the day I got the word her chopper had gone down. We'd had a few stolen moments the night before. In less than a month, both our groups would be leaving Syria. I would be assigned to Camp Pendleton in California and she had orders for Virginia. She had less than a year left and I had a few months longer than that. She was to start planning our wedding."

"I'm sorry, Garth."

He drew in a deep breath. "So am I. For whatever reason you wanted to know about Karen, there you have it. Any other questions?"

"Yes, there is one. Do you stay in touch with her family?"

"Somewhat. Her parents are now deceased, and her older brother followed in his father's footsteps and is a minister in Kansas. I hear from him from time to time."

He didn't say anything for a minute. Then, he said, "I came to let you know breakfast was ready. That seems like ages ago. I'm sure Paulo has kept everything warming." His posture straightened and he moved away from the dresser.

"I'll be showered, dressed and ready to join you at breakfast in twenty minutes."

Garth nodded and was about to leave the room when she called out to him. "Garth?"

He turned around. "Yes?"

"Thanks for sharing that with me."

He nodded again and walked out.

Garth stood at the huge window in the dining room and looked out at the ocean. Today the gusts were high, and the waves were choppy. Regardless, the sea looked beautiful, and this spot was great to view it all. His waterfront home on the Chena River in Fairbanks, even with its rustic appeal, couldn't compare to this.

His lips curved into a smile. Nothing could compare to *Regan*. When he'd walked into the bedroom and seen her in his bed… With the sheet pulled up to cover her breasts and her hair all mussed around her shoulders, she'd looked like a goddess. A sexy, tumbled goddess.

Nothing could erase that image from his mind. Not even the question she'd asked about Karen. A part of him had initially felt Regan didn't have a right to ask anything. But then, when he'd begun talking about Karen, he'd realized he had needed to have that conversation. He wasn't sure why he felt that way, but he had.

Before walking out of the room, he'd come close to asking a question of his own. Was she honestly thinking about taking that job with Anders? Although Charm thought she wasn't, he wanted to hear it from Regan's own lips. However, to ask her about it would reveal where he'd heard it from and all fingers would point to Charm. He'd promised his sister he would keep the information to himself.

His mind filled with thoughts of yesterday. Especially their time in the hot tub. That had been the first time he'd ever made love to a woman in one. After getting out of it, they'd showered together, and ended up in bed making love the entire night. He could get used to this.

Suddenly, it flashed through his mind that no, he could not. Should not. In a few days they would be leaving, and when they did, their affair would end. She knew it and accepted it. No drama. That was the way he wanted it. Their affair had been a mutual, adult decision and was nobody's business. She would return to being his pilot and he her boss.

"Garth?"

He turned at the sound of her voice. If all these sexy outfits she'd been wearing every day were meant to grab his attention, they were working. Today she'd put on what looked to be an island dress that swished around her ankles and hung off her shoulders.

"Yes?"

"I'm ready for breakfast."

She seemed somewhat nervous. Did she assume he was upset because she'd asked him about Karen? If that was the case, he needed to arrest her fears. Crossing the room, he wrapped his arms around her as he looked down at her. "You look beautiful as ever, sweetheart. I love this outfit on you."

Her lips parted into a smile. "Thank you."

"I hope you know I'm wondering about my downfall—"

She lifted a brow. "Your downfall?"

"Yes. I forfeited yesterday's kissing game, so you're the declared winner. That means you get to do whatever you want to me. I hope you take pity on this poor soul."

Her smile widened. "Poor soul? I can't see you falling in that category. I've been thinking of just what I want to do to you, Garth. I've come up with plenty of ideas. Too bad I have to settle on just one."

He took a step closer to her. "Would you like to share that idea with me?"

She took a step back and grinned. "No, and our breakfast is getting cold."

She turned to walk away, and he reached out and pulled her into his arms, leaned in and kissed her. This was his first kiss from her today, but he was going to make sure it wasn't his last. Her taste did something to him each and every time.

When he finally released her mouth, he took her hand and together they headed toward the kitchen.

Eighteen

"Garth, could you come in here a minute, please?"

Regan knew what she intended to do to him would take more than a minute, but she couldn't think of a better way to end their two weeks in Santa Cruz. For as long as she lived, she would always remember the time they'd spent together here. They'd attended a couple more operas, shared dinner at several posh restaurants in town, gone to a movie and taken a drive along several of the scenic beaches. They'd eventually gone hiking in the tropical laurel forests and had spent an entire day kayaking and canoeing.

He'd even gone shopping with her again. They'd bought more souvenirs and she'd helped him find gifts for Walker and Bailey's twins. But no matter what they did during the day, they looked forward to each night when they returned to the château to make love until sleep claimed them. Often, they would awake in the middle of the night and make love again.

She also appreciated how they would spend time talking. Over breakfast Garth would tell her of plans he had to move the company forward, his concern for his father—who still didn't accept that the Westmorelands were related to them—and how finding out about the Westmorelands had enriched his family's lives in many ways. Family meant even more to him now.

He told her about the renovations he intended to make to his home at the beginning of the year, which included adding a theater room. She loved his home and had visited him a number of times with Charm. She especially loved how she could see the Chena River from almost every room.

They'd talked about her father and how he was enjoying life in Florida and how she planned to spend Christmas with him this year. She told Garth about the trip she and Simone had planned to Ireland next year and the renovations she planned to do to her own home. Conversing with him was easy and she enjoyed it tremendously.

Tonight was their last night together. Tomorrow they would leave to return home. He probably assumed she'd forgotten about collecting her reward from the kissing game. If that was what he thought, then he was wrong, because tonight was the night.

A part of her wished they could extend their stay another week, month, year. She had enjoyed being here with him and hoped he had enjoyed being here with her. Her goal had been to make each day memorable for him. Ones he wouldn't forget. Ones he would want to continue, even when they returned to Fairbanks. She wasn't sure if she'd succeeded, but tonight would put the icing on the cake.

Glancing around the room, she saw everything was in place for Garth's hot oil massage. This wouldn't be the first time he'd been in her bedroom, since they'd made love in here for a change in scenery, but at the time the room hadn't looked like this. Tonight she had transformed the bedroom into a romantic sanctuary, complete with burning candles, dim lighting, the scent of lavender and relaxing music. She had set the mood for a night of intense intimacy.

She had taken her time in selecting the oil, glad Garth hadn't been with her at the time. She had talked him into going into a wine shop to select a bottle for their last night together. That was when she had doubled back to a shop that sold everything she needed for tonight. According to the salesclerk, who'd been very knowledgeable, the best scented oil would be lavender. It was relaxing, but also had an arousing effect on a person's mind. She even claimed it stimulated the brain like an aphrodisiac.

Regan looked down at herself. If her outfit didn't get his blood stirring, then nothing would. Garth had no idea what she'd set up for tonight, what her prize would be for winning the kissing contest. What she planned to do to him.

She intended to make it a night he would always remember.

Regan heard the knock on the bedroom door and moved in that direction. He had to be wondering what she'd been doing in here all this time. Maybe he assumed she was packing, since they would be leaving tomorrow.

When she opened the door, he stood there, looking sexier than any man had a right to look. She'd seen him in jeans so much over the past two weeks that it would be hard getting used to him wearing suits again.

"You need me for something?"

Boy, did she ever, she thought, roaming her gaze up and down his masculine form. They hadn't gone out today other than to take a walk around the shore after lunch. Then later, after dinner they had made love, showered and made love again. It was as if they'd wanted to get as much of each other as possible.

And she still wasn't ready to let go, which was why she'd decided to play her last card tonight.

"Yes, come in," she said, stepping aside.

He entered, stopped and did a full circle. Then he looked back at her. "What's going on?" he asked in a husky voice.

"Time for me to collect my kissing game winnings, Garth. I get to do whatever I want with you. And do you know what I plan to do?"

Regan watched his throat move in a deep swallow before he asked, "And just what do you plan to do?"

She moved close to him and rubbed his chest, wishing her fingers could touch his bare skin and not a shirt. "What I want to do to you, Garth Outlaw, is to touch you all over. Tonight, I will be giving you a hot oil massage."

A smile touched his lips. "Bring it on."

Regan returned his smile. "I'm glad you're a willing participant."

"Sweetheart, I don't know a man alive who wouldn't be."

She chuckled. "I need you to undress, Garth. Completely."

Regan stepped back to watch him unbutton his shirt and kick off his shoes. Blood rushed through her veins when her gaze drifted over his open shirt, bare chest and shoeless feet. Then he began shoving his pants and briefs down a pair of masculine legs.

When he was completely nude, she studied every inch of him. He had a body to die for, and she felt she was slowly drawing her last breath. It didn't go unnoticed that while she was ogling him, he was studying her just as intently. Probably wondering what, if anything, she had on under her robe. To appease his curiosity, she wiggled her shoulders to ease out of it and reveal a very sexy negligee.

"Damn, that's nice, Regan. Real nice."

"I'm glad you like it."

And it was so obvious he liked it. There were some things a man couldn't hide. A huge erection was one of them. Knowing she'd caused it was getting to her. "Now I need you to get in the bed and lie facedown, Garth."

She watched him walk over and stretch out on the bed, facedown. At that moment, an intense jolt of sexual need rocked her to the core. She had to get through this. She just had to. She would need the memories of being here with him, freely touching him, long after they'd returned home. She had to accept the reality that no matter what all she'd done here to make him want her, there was a chance he might never think she was wife material because he would never be able to love her. She forced that thought from her mind.

Once he had settled into position, he said, "I can't see you in that short thing you're wearing."

"You will soon enough, Garth."

She studied the contours of his back, which was military straight even while lying down. Coming to stand beside him, she poured heated oil into her hands and began to slowly massage the oil into his skin. There was something about the music playing, the scent of lavender flowing through the room, the low lighting and the gentle flames of the candles. She covered his back from top to bottom, gently rubbing her hands over his buttocks, down his inner and outer thighs, down his legs and all those areas in between.

"That feels so good, baby."

She smiled at that term of endearment. "Trust me, I'm probably getting more out of this than you."

"I doubt it."

What she'd said was true. The feel of her hands gliding across his skin pushed her to succumb to desire that felt like a living creature seeping into her pores, nervous system, the very essence of her mind. It caused an ache in the juncture of her thighs. Her nipples hardened and her heart skipped several beats.

"Now flip over on your back, Garth."

He complied and all she could do was stare at him, letting her gaze roam from the top of his head to the bottoms of his feet. He had beautiful feet for a man. But nothing was more impressive than the huge, engorged erection standing straight up for her. She licked her lips just looking at it.

"Don't do that, sweetheart."

She swallowed and moved her gaze from his midsection to his face. She saw longing so intense in his features that a ball of need burst to life inside her womanly core. Reaching again for the bottle of oil that had been kept in a warmer, she poured an ample amount in her hands.

She gently glided her hands all over his chest, working the oil into his skin, soothing any tense muscles she felt along his shoulders. Then she moved lower, tracing a path down his sculpted abdomen, loving the texture of his skin beneath her fingers.

And when her hands moved lower, their eyes met. She saw desire, more than she'd ever seen before, flare into his eyes. As she took him into her hand, his breathing became choppy.

Not removing her hands, she leaned in close to his mouth and whispered, "Breathe."

When he lifted his hand toward her, she said, "No touching. If you're good, I'll let you touch all you want later. I just want you to lie still and relax."

"You're killing me."

A smile touched her lips. "We are killing each other, and I promise to take us out of our pain real soon."

She moved lower, to his thighs, and began stroking featherlight touches down to his calves. From there she moved to his ankles and the soles of his feet.

After putting more oil in the palms of her hands, she slowly retraced the path up to his shoulders. Once again, she paid a lot of attention to his midsection, letting him know how much she enjoyed touching him there. All kinds of sexual vibes poured off his body.

"Regan…"

She heard the burning sensuality in his voice and saw it in his eyes. The sound and sight made her tremble. "Yes?"

"I need you."

He'd just said he *needed* her, and not just that he *wanted* her. Regan tried not to let his words get to her, but the force of them came crashing down on her when she realized how much she had to gain—and how much she could lose. She refused to think of losing. She had to believe this night and all those other nights meant something to him.

"Regan."

When he said her name again, she leaned close to him and whispered, "You can touch me now."

As if those were the words he'd been waiting for, he quickly sat up and pulled her down on the bed with him. In seconds he had stripped her of her negligee and had her beneath him. He captured her mouth in his at the same time he entered her body in one hard thrust.

She let out a joyous scream and immediately climaxed. The intensity had hot blood rushing through her veins and sexual sensations flooding her stomach. When he threw his head back and let out a guttural moan while pounding hard into her, she screamed again. Another orgasm struck her, more powerful than the one before. He released her mouth and she looked up at him, saw deep-seated pleasure in his eyes. She would always remember putting it there. The questions she forced to the back of her mind were whether or not he would remember. Whether or not she'd done enough to engrave herself into his mind, if not his heart.

"I'm ready to leave, Garth."

Garth tossed aside the magazine he'd been reading and stood. When he glanced over at Regan, he went still. Gone was the sexy temptress who'd been rocking his world for the past two weeks. The woman who'd been his constant companion during the day and shared his bed every night. In her place was Regan, his pilot. Forever the professional. She'd dressed in her uniform to remind him of it. Even her hair was back to being hidden under her pilot's cap. Did she expect him to suddenly stop wanting her just because that uniform was a reminder that he was her boss? Was this her way of letting him know their Santa Cruz fling was officially over?

If that was the way she wanted things to end, then he would give her that wish.

But not until after he'd held her in his arms and tasted her lips one last time.

Crossing the room, he came to a stop in front of her. "I know what happens when we return to Fairbanks, Regan. But we aren't there yet."

He then pulled her into his arms and captured her mouth with his.

Nineteen

Regan dropped down on her sofa as she shifted her cell phone to the other ear. "I'm glad you enjoyed your cruise, Dad. It sounds like you had a great time."

"I did. What about you? That was nice of Garth to invite you to hang out with him in Santa Cruz. Did you enjoy yourself?"

"Yes, I enjoyed myself," she said, easing up from the sofa to cross the room and look out at the lake. Snow was falling. The usual for this time of year. In a week or so, they would be buried in it.

She drew in a deep breath, finding it hard to believe that she and Garth had returned to Fairbanks nearly two weeks ago. She wondered if he'd conveniently forgotten to give her the information about the dating agency that he'd promised her. She had reminded him before they'd left Santa Cruz and again when they'd landed in Fairbanks. He hadn't seemed to like the reminders, but she'd hoped they would light a fire under him.

They had parted at the airport like they usually did, with a "goodbye" and not an "I will see your later." She had checked her calendar, and the next scheduled flight, weather permitting, wasn't until December, when she would fly him to Denver to attend his cousins' charity ball.

Thanksgiving was in a couple of weeks and she'd thought about joining her father then, as well as for Christmas. There was no need to hang around here for the holidays. If Garth had any intention of suggesting they continue to see each other, he would have contacted her by now. Evidently, he had gotten back into his regular routine. For all she knew, he could have started dating again. The thought of that broke her heart, although she shouldn't let it. She had tried to make him see her importance, but obviously her risk hadn't paid off.

Suddenly, she realized she'd been distracted by thoughts of Garth and she'd missed what her father had been saying. She caught the tail end of it. "Excuse me, Dad, but what did you say?"

He gave a soft chuckle. "I said that I met someone. A real nice young lady."

That was what she'd thought he said. Quickly moving away from the window, she returned to the sofa and sat back down. "Young lady? How young, Dad?"

He chuckled again. "She's three years younger than I am, Regan."

Regan was glad to hear that. "You met her on the cruise?"

"No, I met her five months ago and invited her to join me on the cruise."

Regan didn't say anything because she was completely stunned. When she recovered, she said, "You've been seeing someone for five months and didn't tell me? I saw you this summer and you didn't say anything about it."

"I had to be sure, Regan."

She swallowed. "Be sure of what?"

"That Deena was someone I could fall in love with."

Regan swallowed again. "Is she? Have you?"

"Yes. I've fallen in love with her."

She didn't reply. Honestly, she should be happy for her father. She'd been trying to push him into serious relationships for years. She'd given up and thought he would never meet a woman he'd want to give his heart to again. "Tell me about her, Dad."

"Deena is a widow. Her husband died of cancer twelve years ago. She has two sons, both doctors, and a daughter who's a college professor. She's a retired nurse who moved to Florida from Wisconsin. Like me, she wanted to escape cold winters. She moved into the neighborhood around the same time I did, but we met at one of our homeowners' association meetings a year ago. We started out as friends, meeting for coffee and taking walks, and then it moved to something more serious."

Regan nibbled her bottom lip. "I see."

"Well, you don't sound happy for your old man."

"I am happy for you, Dad. Just surprised."

"I can't wait for you to meet her. I told her you were coming here for Christmas."

Regan was about to tell him she might be seeing him sooner than that, when his next words stopped her. "I'm meeting Deena's kids for Thanksgiving. We're flying to Wisconsin, where they live."

Regan didn't respond at first. Then, because she knew how she felt was important to her father, she said, "I am truly happy for you, Dad, and I can't wait to meet Deena when I come visit you for Christmas."

"Thanks, sweetheart. I need to go now. Deena and I have a date later. We're doing dinner and then a movie."

She nodded, hearing the excitement in his voice. "Enjoy yourselves."

"We will. You take care, sweetheart."

"I will, and you do the same, Dad."

After ending the call, Regan stood and walked back over to the window. At least her father had proved that one could love again—although it had taken him nearly twenty years to reach that conclusion. Better late than never. And he honestly sounded happy. She couldn't wait to meet Deena.

Should she take that as hope for herself? She would if Garth had given her any reason for hope when they'd parted at the airport. He hadn't. It was as if once he'd returned to his home turf, she was out of sight and out of mind. She had honestly thought he would have called her by now, if for nothing more than to see how she was doing.

She stood and was about to go into the kitchen when

her phone rang. She quickly picked it up, hoping it was Garth, and then sighed in disappointment when she saw the caller was Charm. "Hey, Charm."

"Hello. I just got back from visiting Walker, Bailey and the twins in Kodiak. The babies are adorable."

"I bet they are, and I bet they are growing like weeds."

Charm chuckled. "Yes, they are. The reason I was calling was to see if you wanted to do dinner tonight at the Riverview? It seems like I haven't seen you in ages, and you need to tell me about Santa Cruz. I'm thinking of taking a trip there myself next summer."

Regan didn't have anything planned for later and getting out of the house to meet Charm was a good idea. "Yes, I'd love to have dinner with you."

Garth stood at the window in his office and looked out. It was hard to believe it had been fourteen days since he'd seen or talked to Regan, and a part of him missed her like crazy. For the past thirteen nights he'd gone to bed remembering how they would shower together, make love, share a bed, and how he would hold her in his arms while she slept and then wake up making love to her every morning.

Those had been the times when he had felt a degree of peace he hadn't felt in ten years. During those two weeks in Santa Cruz, he'd gotten used to being happy, satisfied, at ease with life and comfortable with having Regan around. He'd known her for years, all of her life, and she'd been his pilot for nearly five years, but he could honestly say that during those two weeks, he'd gotten to know her in ways he hadn't thought possible. Not all of it had been spent in the bedroom. However, he would be the first to admit the times in the bedroom had been special.

He'd even opened up and told her about Karen, not knowing how much he'd needed to talk about his past with someone other than Walker. Doing so had placed a lot of things in perspective.

Regan had captured his heart.

He had fallen in love with her.

Garth shook his head, not believing how things had turned out. Maybe he'd fallen in love with her last year when his blinders came off, but he'd been fighting it. He'd been convinced he would be dishonoring Karen's memory to give someone else his heart. It had taken ten years to discover he'd been wrong.

It had taken ten years to accept that losing the person he loved didn't mean losing their memory, as well. To love someone and then grieve for them—that was a transition in life that a number of people went through. Just because he felt emotions for another person didn't diminish what he'd once felt for the woman he'd loved and lost. It was about accepting that it was time to move on.

The relationship he'd shared with Karen had been unique, what he'd needed at the time. Now he was ten years older, and a different type of woman appealed to him. A woman like Regan. He admired everything about her. Her sexiness, her overall view on life and her ability to have fun and encourage him to have fun, as well.

Walker was right about a person's heart expanding to include others, if one was willing to let them in. Garth was willing to let Regan in. He *needed* her in.

It had taken fourteen long, tortuous days and nights to finally accept that. Now that he'd come to terms with the idea that Regan was the woman he loved, he knew it was time to act. There was a chance he would lose her if he didn't do something about it. Even now, she expected him to give her information on that dating service and he didn't intend to do that.

He would do whatever it took to make sure she loved him in return. He would court her properly. Take her to dinners, movies, concerts—prove there was more than sex between them. He'd once told her she deserved a man who would love her, and it was up to him to prove that *he* was that man.

He suddenly felt good. Totally rejuvenated. He would call her, something he'd wanted to do many times since returning, but he had fought against it. He would invite her to dinner tomorrow night. He would take her to someplace super nice.

Garth heard his stomach growl. He had skipped lunch due to a conference call and needed to have dinner. Grabbing his jacket off the coatrack, he was about to leave when his personal assistant beeped him.

"Yes, Helen?"

"Your sister is here to see you."

A smile curved his lips as he replaced his jacket back on the rack. "Please send her in."

A smiling Charm walked in. This was the first time he'd seen her since he'd returned. Cash had told him she'd gone to visit Walker and Bailey in Kodiak. "So, you finally remembered you have a job that you needed to come back to?" he asked, grinning. It was a joke with him and his brothers that Charm worked in spells. They just weren't sure when those spells would hit.

"Oh, stop trying to be a big bad CEO," she said, crossing the room to give him a huge hug. "I missed you."

"And I missed you, too. However, I do need to remind you that you're on the company's payroll and have an office here."

She waved a hand at him as she took the chair in front of his desk. "Whatever. How was Santa Cruz?"

"It was nice," he said, sitting down, as well.

"And did you show Regan how much she was appreciated?"

If only she knew how much, how often and to what extent he'd shown Regan, she wouldn't be asking.

"Yes, I did." Then he decided to quickly change the subject. "So, how's Walker, Bailey and the twins?"

"They are great, and it was fun hanging out with them. I kept Bailey company while Walker flew to Anchorage. I even got to feed the twins. Walker IV and Westlyn are so cute."

Charm looked at her watch and stood. "I need to get going. I'm meeting Regan for dinner."

Garth, who'd been fiddling with a file on his desk, jerked his head up. "You're having dinner with Regan?"

"Yes. I haven't seen her for a while and invited her to dinner. You want to join us? I'm sure she wouldn't mind."

More than anything, he wanted to see Regan again. He was about to tell Charm that yes, he would love to join them, when his personal assistant beeped him again. "Yes, Helen?"

"There's someone here to see you."

"Who?"

"A woman by the name of Josephine Harris."

Josephine Harris?

The woman from the dating service.

He immediately glanced over at Charm. "Did you not cancel my membership with that dating service?"

"I most certainly did," Charm said. "Her being here is breaking that company's policy and procedures. They are to handle any contact between the two of you. I wonder why she's here."

Garth reached for his jacket to put it on. "I don't know but I'm about to find out." He then said to Helen, "Please escort her in."

Josephine Harris was a beautiful woman. He'd known that since he'd seen photos of her. She was sharp, sleek and sophisticated, and looked good in the outfit she was wearing. The two-piece ensemble had the word *class* written all over it.

But she wasn't Regan.

As far as he as concerned, Regan had all those same qualities and more.

"Josephine, this is a surprise."

He then introduced her to Charm and noticed that the two women shook hands and said all the niceties, but he knew his sister well enough to know there was immediate dislike on her end.

He caught Charm's gaze. "Don't you have a dinner date?"

"Yes. I guess I'll be going. I'll talk to you tomorrow."

He nodded. "Okay and please tell Regan I said hello." There was no need to tell Charm to tell Regan he intended to call her later. For now, the less Charm knew the better.

"I'll tell her." She then turned to Josephine. "It was nice meeting you, Josephine."

"Same here, Charm."

The moment the door closed behind his sister, Garth returned his attention to Josephine. "Would you like to have a seat?"

"Yes, thanks." She sat down in the chair Charm had vacated and gracefully crossed her legs. Garth knew this was so he would notice. He had. Only thing, although they were a nice pair, he liked Regan's legs better.

"So, Josephine, why are you here?" he asked, taking a seat behind his desk. "Didn't the dating service notify you that I'm no longer a client with them?"

"Yes, I was advised of that. However, I figured the least we could do was officially meet. So here I am. I believe we would have enjoyed our two weeks together."

Garth had a feeling she might have, but he would not have. He was glad the woman he'd spent two weeks with had been Regan. "Would we have?"

"Yes, and I intend to prove it. I decided to come here to spend some time with you. I'll be here for a week."

She'd decided?

He needed to explain to Josephine Harris that any

involvement they might have looked forward to at one time was no longer a possibility. Granted, he understood the mix-up hadn't been her fault, but now his heart was elsewhere. And for her to assume she could just show up here unannounced, with the expectation that he would make time for her...for a week...was ludicrous.

His brothers' offices were down the hall. They might pop into his at any time and the last thing he wanted to do was explain Josephine Harris to them. He was hungry and decided he would set her straight over dinner.

"How about having dinner with me?" he said.

Her lips curved into a huge smile. Too late he saw she'd taken his invitation as something positive. She would find out soon enough it wasn't.

"I'd love to dine with you, Garth. Then you can tell me if I'll be staying at the hotel for a week or at your place."

Garth stood and grabbed his jacket. Yes, he most certainly would be telling her that and a lot more.

Twenty

"I'm glad you enjoyed yourself in Santa Cruz, Regan."

Regan smiled over at Charm. Like Garth, Charm was known for her radiant smile. Unless she didn't like you, and then she had no problem making that fact known. "Thanks." And because Regan didn't want Charm to ask her any more questions, she decided to change the subject.

"When are you going on your holiday shopping trip?" It was a known fact that Charm traveled to LA around Thanksgiving every year just to do holiday shopping.

"Not sure. I just got back in town and Garth reminded me that I'm getting paid to do a job I'm rarely in the office doing. Like I don't know the only reason they gave me that cushy office and job title was to keep me out of their hair. He told me to tell you hello, by the way."

Regan's fork nearly slipped from her hand. "Did he?"

"Yes. I just left his office before coming here and mentioned I was having dinner with you. I invited him to join us, but that was before…"

Charm's voice trailed off and Regan glanced up from her meal to study her. Charm was staring at something across the room, and the smile that had been on her face earlier was gone. "Charm? What is it?"

"I don't believe it. Garth just walked in, and I can't believe he's actually having dinner with her."

Regan felt her heart drop. "Her who?"

"Josephine Harris. The woman who was supposed to join him in Santa Cruz."

Pain twisted in Regan's chest. "But I thought he'd decided not to reschedule a meeting with her," Regan said. At least that was what he'd told her.

"That's true. I canceled his membership with that dating service myself. But she showed up at his office today, right before I left to come here. He seemed annoyed that she'd showed up unexpectedly like that."

Regan took a sip of her wine. "Well, if they're here for dinner, that means he's no longer annoyed."

"Evidently not. They're being escorted to a table. They can't see us, but we have a good view of them. Look to your right."

Regan did and her heart felt crushed. "She's gorgeous."

Charm rolled her eyes. "Yes, if you like the phony type. I bet everything on her is fake. Her boobs, her hair, her nails. I'm even questioning that outfit. Not all women choose to show off their assets like that."

At any other time, Regan would have found what Charm said amusing, but not now. Not when pain had taken over her body. She'd honestly thought she had a chance with Garth, even after two weeks with no contact, but she was being proven wrong. All it took was seeing how the woman clung to Garth while being led to their table.

"Regan? Are you all right?"

She looked back at Charm and wondered why she'd asked. Had the tears she was trying so hard to fight been forming in her eyes anyway? "I'm fine, Charm."

Even when she spoke the words, she knew they were a lie, and she had a feeling Charm knew, as well.

Garth arrived at the office early the next morning because he and his brothers had a meeting scheduled at nine. Over dinner he'd finally gotten through to Josephine Harris. He was not interested in her. The woman had honestly thought a lot of herself. Had placed herself on a pedestal so high he'd gotten a crick in his neck looking up at her.

As soon as this morning's meeting was over, he would call Regan and invite her to dinner tonight. He would have contacted her last night, but it was late when he'd gotten in, and after dealing with Josephine, he hadn't been in the best of moods.

A short while later, he entered the conference room and found his brothers all there. As was Charm. He didn't recall inviting her to the meeting. And why did they all have serious looks on their faces?

"Good morning, everyone."

He was quick to note the greeting had not been returned. "Is there a problem?"

"We think so," Cash said, sliding an envelope to the middle of the table.

Garth lifted a brow. "What's this?"

"Why don't you read it and see?" Sloan said, and his voice had a sharp edge to it.

Garth wondered what the hell was going on. He picked up the envelope, opened it and read the document. He snatched his head up and saw four accusing pair of eyes staring him down.

"Regan is resigning."

"Apparently, and we want to know why," Sloan said in an irritated voice.

"What happened during those two weeks she stayed with you in Santa Cruz?" Maverick asked angrily.

Cash's gaze snapped around to Maverick. "Regan was with him the entire time?" he asked, making it obvious that this was the first he'd heard of it.

"Yes, she was with him the entire time," Charm said, in a disgusted voice. "I suggested he ask her to join him there as a way to show how much he appreciated her." She then turned her attention back to her oldest brother. "So, what happened in Santa Cruz, Garth?"

Garth narrowed his gaze at his four siblings. What they were asking was none of their damn business. But because he knew how much Regan meant to them, he would tell them what they wanted to know.

Placing his hands on the table and leaning on his arms, he faced them down. "Since the four of you want to know something that's really none of your business, I will tell you exactly what happened with me and Regan in Santa Cruz. I fell in love with her."

From the shocked look on his siblings' faces, his response hadn't been what they'd expected.

"You fell in love with Regan?" The question was asked from four sets of lips.

"Yes, I fell in love with her. I honestly believe I fell in love with her last year at the Westmoreland Charity Ball, but it took me this long to accept it."

"Hell, I suspected something was up," Cash said, a grin replacing his scowl. "You were acting so territorial that night and I figured it had to be for a reason."

"I suspected the same," Sloan said and Maverick nodded to agree.

"Not so fast," Charm said, tossing her hands in the air as if she wasn't buying what he'd said as easily as her brothers. "If you love Regan, then explain last night."

Garth frowned. "Last night?"

"Yes, last night. Regan and I were having dinner at the Riverview when you and that Josephine Harris woman arrived."

Garth drew in a deep breath. "Damn." He recalled how Josephine had clung to him walking into the restaurant, wanting to make it seem like they were an item.

"Who is Josephine Harris?" Maverick wanted to know.

"The woman from the dating agency," Charm answered.

"What dating agency?" Sloan asked.

Garth ignored his question. Instead he kept his gaze trained on Charm. "I took Josephine Harris to dinner to tell her I didn't want to see her again."

"Well, it didn't look that way from where Regan and I sat. The woman was practically all over you. I would not have known that seeing you and the woman together bothered Regan if I didn't know her so well. And then when she called me this morning to say she was resigning and to make sure you got her note, that's when I put two and two together."

Garth straightened and shoved the envelope into the pocket of his jacket. "This meeting is canceled."

He then walked out briskly.

Regan stood back and studied the Christmas tree she'd just decorated. Granted, Thanksgiving was still two weeks away, but it didn't matter to her. She loved the holidays, Christmas especially. Besides, she needed to do something to keep her busy, to keep her from thinking about Garth. She checked her watch. He should have gotten her resignation letter by now.

She had cried herself to sleep last night, after calling herself all kinds of fool for thinking it would be easy to win him over. And what was even more pathetic was that she hadn't even gone after his heart. She'd figured desire would be the foundation and that one day he would eventually fall in love with her. She'd been willing to take that chance.

But things hadn't worked out that way, and it was time to move on to protect her heart. After all that time they'd spent together and what they'd shared—if Josephine Harris could easily walk in and erase it from his mind, then the woman was welcome to him.

He wouldn't need a pilot until the end of next month, which gave him plenty of time to look for her replacement. She would call Harold Anders later today and accept his job offer. Also, later today she would call her father and let him know of her decision to resign. For the first time in over forty years, a Fairchild would not be the corporate pilot for Outlaw Freight Lines. She would make both of those calls later. Right now, she wanted to stand here, sip her coffee and stare at her beautifully decorated Christmas tree.

Her doorbell sounded. She frowned, wondering who would be paying her a visit. She hoped it wasn't Charm. Last night she'd come close to spilling her guts.

Leaving the living room, she went to the door. "Who is it?"

"Garth."

Garth? What was he doing here?

If he thought he could talk her out of resigning, then he was wrong. But more than anything, she would not let him think the reason she was quitting had anything to do with him…even if it did. She had her pride.

She opened the door and pasted a cheery smile on her face. "Garth? What are you doing here?"

"May I come in?"

"Sure." She stepped aside to let him in.

He'd been to her house before, many times, when he'd been kind enough to pick her up for the airport because of bad weather. This was the first time she'd noticed how his tall, muscular frame seemed to take up a large portion of her living room.

"That's a pretty Christmas tree."

She followed his gaze. "Thanks." She then looked back at him. "Why are you here, Garth?"

He pulled an envelope out of his coat pocket. "About this. We need to talk, Regan."

She lifted her chin. "Why? I resigned. There's nothing to talk about. I got a better job offer, and I'm taking it. End of story."

"I don't think that's the end of the story. We should talk."

Regan drew in a deep breath. She had given two weeks' notice, so technically he was still her boss for now. She would listen to what he had to say, and then she would ask him to leave. There was nothing he could say that would make her change her mind at this point.

"Fine. We'll talk. May I take your coat?" She watched him peel his coat off massive shoulders and a masculine body. A body she had tasted all over, straddled, laid hands on…

"Here you are."

She blinked, knowing he'd caught her staring. Fighting to regain control of her senses, she took the coat from him. "I'll be back after hanging it up."

When she returned, he was standing in front of the tree. As always, he looked good in his business suit, but she liked him in jeans, too. "So, let's talk, Garth."

He turned around and met her gaze, and she nearly got weak in the knees. He was staring at her the way he'd stared at her a number of times in Santa Cruz.

There was so much desire in his dark eyes. She took a deep breath. She honestly didn't have time for any of his lusty dispatches. "Please say what you have to say, then leave, Garth."

He nodded. "I'm not accepting your resignation," he said, tossing the envelope on a nearby table.

She crossed her arms over her chest. "You don't have a choice. I've accepted another job that's paying me more."

"That's not the reason you're quitting and you know it. Charm said the two of you were at the Riverview for dinner yesterday."

"And what of it?"

"I think you got the wrong impression."

She rolled her eyes. "I have no idea what you're talking about. You're free to dine wherever you want and with whomever you want. My resignation has nothing to do with that."

"I don't believe you, Regan."

"You think a whole lot of yourself if you believe my wanting to advance my career has anything to do with you. I'd gotten that job offer weeks ago and was trying to decide whether I should take it or not. I've decided. Sorry my decision doesn't meet with your approval."

"Why are you doing this to us?"

"Us?" That one word made her snap. "There was never an us, Garth. I knew it and I accepted it, yet I'd come up with this brilliant idea, using all that strategy planning I've watched you use over the years. I figured if I could be the woman you wanted, then I could certainly become the wife you needed. Stupid me for thinking such a thing was possible. I was even willing to let love come later or not at all. But my plan backfired. After I gave you those two weeks, you weren't satisfied. I wish you the best with your perfect woman and I hope you wish me the same with my employer."

She hadn't meant to go off on him and say as much as she had. But it was too late to take any of it back.

"Now please leave, Garth, and take my resignation letter with you, because it's official."

Twenty-One

Instead of leaving like she requested, Garth moved away from the Christmas tree, took off his suit jacket and placed it across the back of her sofa. Then he rolled up his shirtsleeves.

"And just what do you think you're doing?"

"I'm about to fight, Regan. Not with you but *for* you. While growing up, I resented Bart for not fighting for my mom when my parents split. He never fought for her. He just fought her for me. I don't plan to make that same mistake."

Garth paused and then said, "Yesterday morning, after thirteen sleepless nights of pure hell, I woke up ready to admit the truth. That you had somehow done something no woman was supposed to do after Karen. You had somehow wiggled your way into my heart."

She shook her head as if what he'd said was too far-fetched to believe. "No, I did not."

He held up his hand. "Hold up. You had your say and now it's time I had mine."

He was glad she tightened her lips so he could continue. "I had made up my mind to call you last night and ask if I could take you out to dinner, so I could tell you everything. Especially what I felt in my heart. Then, unexpectedly, the woman who was supposed to meet me in Santa Cruz showed up, assuming we could hang out together for a week to make up for the time we didn't get in Spain."

He paused to draw in a deep breath. "The reason I took her to dinner was because I skipped lunch and was hungry. And I honestly didn't want to burst her bubble on an empty stomach, and I didn't want my brothers questioning me about the woman in my office. She broke the dating service's ironclad policy by even seeking me out. You of all people know what a stickler I am for people following the rules."

"But she's gorgeous."

"So are you. No comparison in my book," he said.

"She was all over you."

Garth heard the hurt in her voice. "But at any time did you see me all over her? I knew who I wanted, and nothing she said or did would have made me change my mind. I considered her of no significance."

He walked across the room to stand in front of Regan. "You're a different story. There were a number of things I had to overcome, and you helped me do that. I loved Karen and for years I refused to feel those same emotions for anyone else. However, you showed me that it was okay to be happy in a new relationship. And being happy didn't mean I was forgetting or replacing feelings I had for the person I lost. It meant I had discovered how to tuck those feelings into a special place in my heart and move on."

"What are you saying, Garth?"

He took a step closer to Regan. "What I'm trying to say is that I love you, Regan. I believe I fell in love with you at the Westmoreland Charity Ball. I told you why I even used that dating service in the first place. The more I saw you, the more I desired you. I figured that if I turned my attention to another woman, that would solve the problem because I honestly didn't think I could give you the love you deserve. Now I know I can."

A smile spread across his lips. "Whatever strategy you used on me worked. I love you and will continue to say it until you believe me, Regan. Yes, it took me fourteen days since we've been back to accept it. Go ahead and count it against me as being slow. But it has no bearing on the depth of my love for you. I love you, and I will spend the rest of my life showing you how much."

He saw the tears stream down her face and then she said, "And I love you, too. I've loved you forever."

Her words surprised him. She'd said she'd wanted him for a long time but had never said how long. "You have?"

She wiped away her tears. "Yes. The reason I returned to Fairbanks after just one year at the university in Los Angeles was not because of Dad. It was because of you."

He lifted a brow. "Me?"

"Yes. Even when I knew you were hurting after losing Karen, I still wanted to be there for you."

Her words touched him deeply. "I never knew. I love you so much." He reached out and pulled her into his arms, then lowered his mouth to hers.

Twenty-Two

"The decorating committee has outdone itself this year," Garth said, glancing around.

Regan thought the same thing. The ballroom of the Pavilion Hotel was absolutely gorgeous and set the stage for another Westmoreland Charity Ball. And because this was also New Year's Eve, everyone was in a festive mood and excited for the arrival of the new year.

She was one of those people.

So much had happened since that day in November when Garth had shown up at her home, refusing to accept her resignation and then proclaiming his love for her. Afterward, he'd called the office to inform Cash and the others he was taking the rest of the day off. He'd ended up taking the next three days off when he'd insisted they fly to Kodiak to visit Walker, Bailey and the twins.

Regan had spent Thanksgiving with the Outlaws and there was no doubt in anyone's mind, including Bart's, as to what type of relationship Regan and Garth shared. Then they'd spent Christmas with her father and met Deena. Regan liked her immediately and concluded the attractive woman was everything her father needed. He seemed truly happy.

"You're quiet."

She glanced up at Garth and smiled. He looked handsome in his tux. "I was just thinking about Dad and how happy he is."

"Yes, Franklin is happy and I'm happy for him. I hope you slept well last night."

Regan nearly choked on her punch and glanced up at him grinning. "Who slept?" she asked, knowing he'd kept her up most of the night making love.

Jason Westmoreland's wife, Bella, had renovated her ranch house into a bed-and-breakfast inn to be used by visiting relatives and business associates. Garth and all his siblings, as well as some of the visiting Westmorelands from Atlanta, Montana and Texas, were all staying at the inn.

Regan had met a lot of the Westmorelands at last year's charity ball. None of them seemed surprised to discover that she and Garth were now an item. Some of the ladies claimed they'd noted an attraction between them at the last ball.

A couple of hours later, Charm and Bailey came to grab Regan from Garth's side. "There's one of those photo booths downstairs. Let's take a picture together," Bailey said, grinning.

"Okay."

There was a line when they got there, and a number of the Westmoreland ladies were there to take pictures in the booth, as well. Someone suggested a group photo and several individual and duo shots. Regan figured a full hour had passed and was surprised Garth hadn't come looking for her. She glanced at her watch. Midnight would be in less than a half hour.

The first thing she noticed when she returned to the ballroom was that it was completely dark. "I wonder what happened?" Regan whispered to Charm.

"I have no idea," was Charm's response.

Suddenly a bright light came on—a spotlight. And it was shining directly on her.

"What in the world?" she turned to ask Charm and Bailey, only to discover they were no longer by her side.

Then, unexpectedly, another group of lights came on. A portion of the dance floor was lit by candlelight in the shape of a huge heart. Regan was certain she had never seen anything so beautiful. Then, with the magic of a hologram, special effects and enhanced sound, a private jet landed in the center of the ballroom floor. Suddenly the cabin door of the jet in the hologram image appeared to open, and there stood Garth. He glanced over to where she was before walking toward her with a single red rose in his hand.

She couldn't stop the tears from falling when he stopped in front of her and presented her with the rose. Then, putting her arm in the crook of his, he walked her over to where the candlelit heart illuminated the dance floor.

Once they were there, a microphone was placed in Garth's hand. "I have a special dance for us, but first let me introduce the members of the band. We'll have Dillon and Micah Westmoreland with their guitars; Bane Westmoreland on keyboard; Riley Westmoreland on the piano; Canyon Westmoreland with his French horn; Jason Westmoreland and his saxophone; and Stern Westmoreland with his violin. The band will be conducted by the renowned Sampson Kilburn, who was once their music instructor. He credits their mother, Clarisse, an accomplished pianist in her own right, with making sure all seven of her sons had an ear for music."

The onlookers went wild when the seven Westmorelands took their place on stage with their instruments. With Sampson conducting, the lights dimmed again. The music began playing and Garth drew her into his arms.

Regan was still speechless as she gazed up into Garth's smiling face. They were dancing inside the heart-shaped area. For the past two months Garth had done everything in his power to show her how much she was loved. At night they rarely stayed apart, and every day he showed her how vital he thought she was in his life.

When the music ended, she watched as he lowered himself to one knee and gazed up into her eyes. "Just so you know, I got your father's permission to do this," he said, taking a small box out of his jacket. "I love you, Regan. Will you marry me?"

More tears appeared in Regan's eyes. "Yes, Garth, I will marry you." She felt a ring slide onto her finger. Glancing down, she saw the huge, sparkling diamond. It was beautiful and so radiant it was blinding.

He got to his feet and pulled her into his arms for a passionate kiss as the Westmoreland band started performing again.

Epilogue

A beautiful day in June

"Garth, you may kiss your bride."

Garth had wondered if the minister would ever get to that part. He was ready. He smiled when he pulled Regan into his arms and lowered his mouth to hers. After Walker, who'd been his best man, nudged him in the side, Garth released her mouth. It was then that they turned to face all three hundred guests as the minister said, "I present to everyone Garth and Regan Outlaw."

Cheers went up and he figured it was a good time to kiss his wife again. Turning her to him, he took her into his arms again to do just that.

An hour or so later, after the photographer had taken a ton of pictures, he and Regan were making their way around the huge ballroom of the Pyramid Hotel in downtown Fairbanks. It was beautiful. After he'd told Regan how Riley's wife, Alpha, who was a party planner, and Dillon's movie star sister-law, Paige Novak, and several of her Hollywood friends had put together the theatrics for his proposal, Regan had been quick to hire Alpha as her wedding planner. Regan had chosen the storybook wedding theme and Alpha had delivered.

The Westmorelands were there in huge numbers, and when they saw Bart for the first time, the Denver group was shocked by how much he favored their fathers, Adam and Tomas. Of course, Bart was still in denial, although last night at the rehearsal dinner he'd tapped Riley on the shoulder, thinking he was Garth. Charm's mother, Claudia, the love of Bart's life, had arrived a few days ago for the wedding, and thankfully, Bart was on his best behavior.

"Hey, Garth, Regan."

They turned to face several of the Atlanta Westmorelands. "There is a bet going on as to which of you will be flying the jet to your honeymoon," Storm Westmoreland said.

Garth shook his head. The one thing he knew about his Westmoreland cousins was that they enjoyed betting and gambling as much as the Outlaws.

"Really?" he asked, ignoring Regan's chuckle.

"Yes, so who's it going to be?" Durango Westmoreland asked.

Garth shook his head. He and Regan would be leaving first thing in the morning for their honeymoon in the Netherlands. "I'll let my wife answer that."

All pair of eyes shifted to Regan, who said, "We both will."

"Okay, guys, pay up." Not surprisingly, it was Ian who won the money.

When they walked off, Garth glanced down at Regan and brought their joined hands to his lips. "Have I told you lately that I love you?"

"Only once since I became Mrs. Outlaw."

He threw his head back and laughed before leaning close and whispering in her ear. "I love you, Regan."

She beamed up at him with what he thought was the sexiest smile ever when she said, "I love you, too, and thanks for making me the wife you need."

* * * * *

Look for Cash Outlaw's story,
coming in April 2021!
The Marriage He Demands

**WE HOPE YOU ENJOYED
THIS BOOK FROM**

DESIRE

*Luxury, scandal, desire—welcome to
the lives of the American elite.*

Be transported to the worlds of oil barons, family dynasties,
moguls and celebrities. Get ready for juicy plot twists,
delicious sensuality and intriguing scandal.

6 NEW BOOKS AVAILABLE EVERY MONTH!

HDHALO2020

COMING NEXT MONTH FROM

DESIRE

Available January 12, 2021

#2779 THE RANCHER'S WAGER
Gold Valley Vineyards • by Maisey Yates
No one gets under Jackson Cooper's skin like Cricket Maxfield. When he goes all in at a charity poker match, Jackson loses their bet and becomes her reluctant ranch hand. In close quarters, tempers flare—and the fire between them ignites into a passion that won't be ignored...

#2780 ONE NIGHT IN TEXAS
Texas Cattleman's Club: Rags to Riches • by Charlene Sands
Gracie Diaz once envied the Wingate family—and wanted Sebastian Wingate. Now she's wealthy in her own right—and pregnant with his baby! Was their one night all they'll ever have? Or is there more to Sebastian than she's ever known?

#2781 THE RANCHER
Dynasties: Mesa Falls • by Joanne Rock
Ranch owner Miles Rivera is surprised to see a glamourous woman like Chiara Campagna in Mesa Falls. When he catches the influencer snooping, he's determined to learn what she's hiding. But when suspicion turns to seduction, can they learn to trust one another?

#2782 RUNNING AWAY WITH THE BRIDE
Nights at the Mahal • by Sophia Singh Sasson
Billionaire Ethan Connors crashes his ex's wedding, only to find he's run off with the wrong bride! Divya Singh didn't want to marry and happily leaves with the sexy stranger. But when their fun fling turns serious, can he win over this runaway bride?

#2783 SCANDAL IN THE VIP SUITE
Miami Famous • by Nadine Gonzalez
Looking for the ultimate getaway, writer Nina Taylor is shocked when *her* VIP suite is given to Hollywood bad boy Julian Knight. Their attraction is undeniable, and soon they've agreed to share the room... and the only bed. But will the meddling press ruin everything?

#2784 INTIMATE NEGOTIATIONS
Blackwells of New York • by Nicki Night
Investment banker Zoe Baldwin is determined to make it in the city's thriving financial industry, but when she meets her handsome new boss, Ethan Blackwell, it's hard to keep things professional. As long days turn into hot nights, can their relationship withstand the secrets between them?

YOU CAN FIND MORE INFORMATION ON UPCOMING HARLEQUIN TITLES, FREE EXCERPTS AND MORE AT HARLEQUIN.COM.

HDCNM1220

SPECIAL EXCERPT FROM

⊕ HARLEQUIN
DESIRE

*No one gets under Jackson Cooper's skin like
Cricket Maxfield. When he goes all in at a charity
poker match, Jackson loses their bet and becomes her
reluctant ranch hand. In close quarters, tempers
flare—and the fire between them ignites into a
passion that won't be ignored...*

Read on for a sneak peek at
The Rancher's Wager
by New York Times *bestselling author Maisey Yates!*

Cricket Maxfield had a hell of a hand. And her confidence made
that clear. Poor little thing didn't think she needed a poker face if
she had a hand that could win.

But he knew better.

She was sitting there with his hat, oversize and over her eyes, on
her head and an unlit cigar in her mouth.

A mouth that was disconcertingly red tonight, as she had clearly
conceded to allowing her sister Emerson to make her up for the
occasion. That bulky, fringed leather jacket should have looked
ridiculous, but over that red dress, cut scandalously low, giving a
tantalizing wedge of scarlet along with pale, creamy cleavage, she
was looking not ridiculous at all.

And right now, she was looking like far too much of a winner.

Lucky for him, around the time he'd escalated the betting, he'd
been sure she would win.

He'd wanted her to win.

"I guess that makes you my ranch hand," she said. "Don't worry.
I'm a very good boss."

Now, Jackson did not want a boss. Not at his job, and not in his
bedroom. But her words sent a streak of fire through his blood. Not
because he wanted her in charge. But because he wanted to show
her what a boss looked like.

Cricket was…

A nuisance. If anything.

That he had any awareness of her at all was problematic enough. Much less that he had any awareness of her as a woman. But that was just because of what she was wearing. The truth of the matter was, Cricket would turn back into the little pumpkin she usually was once this evening was over and he could forget all about the fact that he had ever been tempted to look down her dress during a game of cards.

"Oh, I'm sure you are, sugar."

"I'm your boss. Not your sugar."

"I wasn't aware that you winning me in a game of cards gave you the right to tell me how to talk."

"If I'm your boss, then I definitely have the right to tell you how to talk."

"Seems like a gray area to me." He waited for a moment, let the word roll around on his tongue, savoring it so he could really, really give himself all the anticipation he was due. "Sugar."

"We're going to have to work on your attitude. You're insubordinate."

"Again," he said, offering her a smile, "I don't recall promising a specific attitude."

There was activity going on around him. The small crowd watching the game was cheering, enjoying the way this rivalry was playing out in front of them. He couldn't blame them. If the situation wasn't at his expense, then he would have probably been smirking and enjoying himself along with the rest of the audience, watching the idiot who had lost to the little girl with the cigar.

He might have lost the hand, but he had a feeling he'd win the game.

Don't miss what happens next in…
The Rancher's Wager
by New York Times *bestselling author Maisey Yates!*

Available January 2021 wherever
Harlequin Desire books and ebooks are sold.

Harlequin.com

Copyright © 2021 by Maisey Yates

HDEXP1220

Get 4 FREE REWARDS!

We'll send you 2 FREE Books plus 2 FREE Mystery Gifts.

Harlequin Desire® books transport you to the world of the American elite with juicy plot twists, delicious sensuality and intriguing scandal.

FREE Value Over **$20**

YES! Please send me 2 FREE Harlequin Desire novels and my 2 FREE gifts (gifts are worth about $10 retail). After receiving them, if I don't wish to receive any more books, I can return the shipping statement marked "cancel." If I don't cancel, I will receive 6 brand-new novels every month and be billed just $4.55 per book in the U.S. or $5.24 per book in Canada. That's a savings of at least 13% off the cover price! It's quite a bargain! Shipping and handling is just 50¢ per book in the U.S. and $1.25 per book in Canada.* I understand that accepting the 2 free books and gifts places me under no obligation to buy anything. I can always return a shipment and cancel at any time. The free books and gifts are mine to keep no matter what I decide.

225/326 HDN GNND

Name (please print)

Address   Apt. #

City   State/Province   Zip/Postal Code

Email: Please check this box ☐ if you would like to receive newsletters and promotional emails from Harlequin Enterprises ULC and its affiliates. You can unsubscribe anytime.

Mail to the **Reader Service:**
IN U.S.A.: P.O. Box 1341, Buffalo, NY 14240-8531
IN CANADA: P.O. Box 603, Fort Erie, Ontario L2A 5X3

Want to try 2 free books from another series? Call 1-800-873-8635 or visit www.ReaderService.com.

---

*Terms and prices subject to change without notice. Prices do not include sales taxes, which will be charged (if applicable) based on your state or country of residence. Canadian residents will be charged applicable taxes. Offer not valid in Quebec. This offer is limited to one order per household. Books received may not be as shown. Not valid for current subscribers to Harlequin Desire books. All orders subject to approval. Credit or debit balances in a customer's account(s) may be offset by any other outstanding balance owed by or to the customer. Please allow 4 to 6 weeks for delivery. Offer available while quantities last.

Your Privacy—Your information is being collected by Harlequin Enterprises ULC, operating as Reader Service. For a complete summary of the information we collect, how we use this information and to whom it is disclosed, please visit our privacy notice located at corporate.harlequin.com/privacy-notice. From time to time we may also exchange your personal information with reputable third parties. If you wish to opt out of this sharing of your personal information, please visit readerservice.com/consumerschoice or call 1-800-873-8635. **Notice to California Residents**—Under California law, you have specific rights to control and access your data. For more information on these rights and how to exercise them, visit corporate.harlequin.com/california-privacy.

HD20R2

Love Harlequin romance?

DISCOVER.

Be the first to find out about promotions, news and exclusive content!

f Facebook.com/HarlequinBooks

🐦 Twitter.com/HarlequinBooks

📷 Instagram.com/HarlequinBooks

📌 Pinterest.com/HarlequinBooks

ReaderService.com

EXPLORE.

Sign up for the Harlequin e-newsletter and download a free book from any series at **TryHarlequin.com**

CONNECT.

Join our Harlequin community to share your thoughts and connect with other romance readers!
Facebook.com/groups/HarlequinConnection

HSOCIAL2020